ALSO BY HELEN FROST

Keesha's House

Spinning Through the Universe

The Braid

Diamond Willow

Crossing Stones

Hidden

SALT

HELEN FROST

SALT

A Story of Friendship in a Time of War

Frances Foster Books
Farrar Straus Giroux
New York

Farrar Straus Giroux Books for Young Readers
175 Fifth Avenue, New York 10010

Designed by Jay Colvin
Printed in the United States of America
First edition, 2013
1   3   5   7   9   10   8   6   4   2

mackids.com

Library of Congress Cataloging-in-Publication Data
Frost, Helen, date.
    Salt / Helen Frost. — 1st ed.
        p.   cm.
    Summary: Twelve-year-olds Anikwa, of the Miami village of Kekionga, and
James, of the trading post outside Fort Wayne, find their friendship threatened
by the rising fear and tension brought by the War of 1812.
    ISBN 978-0-374-36387-1 (hardcover)
    ISBN 978-0-374-36388-8
    [1. Novels in verse.   2. Frontier and pioneer life—Indiana—Fiction.
3. Friendship—Fiction.   4. Miami Indians—Fiction.   5. Indians of North America—
Indiana—Fiction.   6. Trading posts—Fiction.   7. Fort Wayne (Ind.)—Fiction.
8. United States—History—War of 1812—Fiction.]   I. Title.

PZ7.5.F76Sal 2013
[Fic]—dc23
                                                                            2012029521

Frontispiece map art by Laszlo Kubinyi. Map research assistance from the Myaamia
Center at Miami University, which consulted Helen Hornbeck Tanner and Miklos
Pinther's *Atlas of Great Lakes Indian History*, pages 96–121.

Farrar Straus Giroux Books for Young Readers may be purchased for business or
promotional use. For information on bulk purchases please contact Macmillan Corporate
and Premium Sales Department at (800) 221-7945 x5442 or by email at specialmarkets@
macmillan.com.

For
Frances Foster
salt of the earth
beloved editor
and friend

"We told each other that we would in future be friends, doing all the good we could to each other, and raise our children in peace and quietness."

Mihšihkinaahkwa, Miami Chief (Little Turtle)
to William H. Harrison, Governor of the Indiana Territory
September 4, 1811

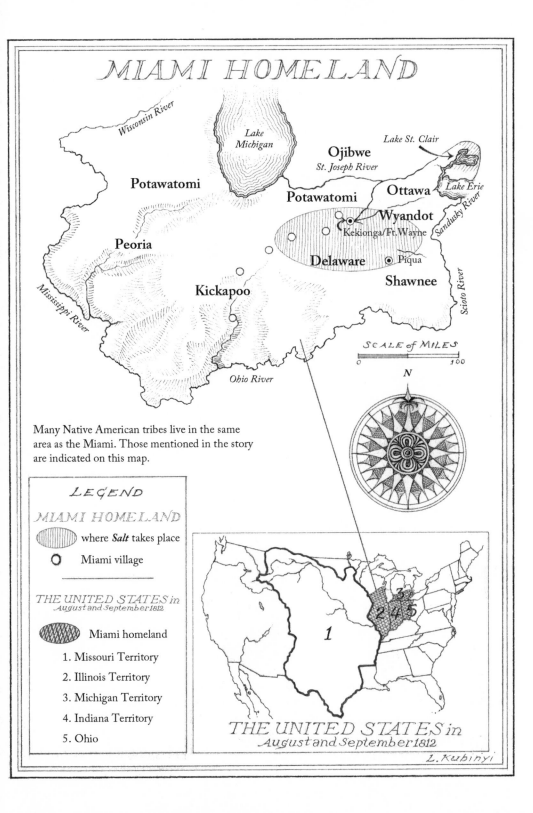

MIAMI HOMELAND

Wisconsin River

Lake Michigan

Ojibwe
St. Joseph River

Lake St. Clair

Lake Erie

Potawatomi

Potawatomi

Ottawa

Wyandot
Kekionga/Ft.Wayne

Sandusky River

Peoria

Delaware

Piqua

Shawnee

Scioto River

Mississippi River

Kickapoo

Ohio River

SCALE of MILES
0   100

N

Many Native American tribes live in the same
area as the Miami. Those mentioned in the story
are indicated on this map.

LEGEND

MIAMI HOMELAND

where *Salt* takes place

O   Miami village

THE UNITED STATES in
August and September 1812

Miami homeland

1. Missouri Territory
2. Illinois Territory
3. Michigan Territory
4. Indiana Territory
5. Ohio

THE UNITED STATES in
August and September 1812

L. Kubinyi

INTRODUCTION

In the summer of 1812, at a place where three rivers meet, the sky is filled with birds of many kinds and colors. The rivers are home to fish, beavers, turtles, and otters. In the forest are deer, bears, wolves, porcupines, foxes, bobcats, squirrels, and rabbits. There is no electricity; there are no telephones. Transportation is by horseback, boat, or on foot over rough roads and trails.

In this time and place, two communities live side by side:

Kekionga is part of the Miami nation, a Native American community made up of villages along the rivers. People have lived in Kekionga for many generations, hunting, fishing, and farming as the seasons change.

Within walking distance of Kekionga, in a fort built with logs, lives a group of about eighty soldiers, sent by the United States government as part of an effort to claim the land and protect the people who are settling on it. Some of the soldiers' wives and children also live in the fort, which is called Fort Wayne. A few other families live outside the fort, within an area enclosed by a wood stockade. Inside this enclosure are fields where the soldiers and their families raise farm animals and crops. Hunting and fishing in the rivers and forest outside the stockade are important to this community, too.

Just inside the stockade, near the gate, is a trading post, and beside the trading post is the home of the trader and his family.

Although there is sometimes distrust and fighting between the two communities, friendships and intermarriage are also common. For a few hundred years, there has been communication and trade between the Miami people and the French, British, and, more recently, Americans.

Please imagine that Anikwa and his family are speaking Miami, a Native American language (today the name of the language is spelled "Myaamia"; the name

"Miami" has nothing to do with present-day Miami, Florida), and James and his family are speaking English. Each child knows a few words and phrases of the other's language, and some of the adults can speak both languages.

A glossary at the back of the book gives definitions of Miami names and words, a guide to their pronunciation, and the address of a Web site where you can hear them spoken.

At the time of this story, the border between the United States and Canada has not been established; the British and American armies are engaged in what will later be called the War of 1812. Tribal leaders of surrounding areas are seeking to create a Confederation of Tribes that would keep land to the north and west of the Ohio River as their nation, separate from the newly formed United States.

The characters in *Salt* are fictional, but the historical events did happen to people who lived in Kekionga and Fort Wayne in late August and early September of 1812.

CHARACTERS

Names in Native American languages have been suggested by tribal members who speak the languages. As was common in 1812, I have kept some names in the original language, and used English translations for others.

Anikwa—Twelve-year-old boy, Miami

Old Raccoon—Anikwa calls him Father. He is Anikwa's father's younger brother, and in the way Miami people think of family, as a close male relative, he is considered to be Anikwa's father

Mink—Old Raccoon's wife

Wiinicia—Old Raccoon's mother; Anikwa calls her Grandma

Rain Bird—Fourteen-year-old girl, daughter of Old Raccoon and Mink, considered an older sister to Anikwa

Toontwa—Six-year-old boy, son of Old Raccoon and Mink, considered a younger brother to Anikwa

Kwaahkwa—Sixteen-year-old boy who lives in Kekionga

Wedaase—Ottawa man who comes to Kekionga

Piyeeto—Shawnee man who has lived in Kekionga for some time

James Gray—Twelve-year-old boy, American, lives outside the fort, within the stockade, in a house near the trading post

Lydia Gray—James's mother

Joseph Gray—James's father, a trader

Molly Gray—James's baby sister

Isaac Briggs—Eleven-year-old boy, lives in the fort

Mr. and Mrs. Briggs—Isaac's father (a soldier) and mother

Becca Briggs—Isaac's younger sister

SALT IN THE SEA, SALT ON THE EARTH

A shallow sea
moves over the earth,
salty, sun-warmed.
Water rises
as mist,
fog, clouds,
leaving a thin coat
of salt on the ground.

JAMES

Dang mosquito bit me right where I can't reach it.
I rub my back against a hickory tree—up and down,

side to side. There—almost got it. Might look silly,
but nobody's watching. Except a squirrel—I hear it

up there in the branches, and I get out my slingshot.
Ma will be happy when I bring home something

for the soup pot. Where is that old squirrel, anyhow?
Sounds like a whole family of 'em, laughing at me,

and I can't see even one. What? Not again! It's
Anikwa, laughing as he jumps down from the tree

and lands beside me. How long has he been watching?
I swear he can sound like anything! Squirrel, bumblebee,

bluebird, or bullfrog. Once, I heard my baby sister crying,
but when I turned to look—it wasn't Molly, it was him!

ANIKWA

James looks
up in the tree like he thinks
there's a real squirrel hiding somewhere
in its branches. I suck in my cheeks
to make myself stop laughing—
he shakes his head,
puts away
his stone and slingshot,
gives me a smile that means I got him
this time, but next time he'll be watching if I
try that trick again. *Come on,* he motions as he heads
to the berry bushes. I've seen him out here picking berries
every afternoon since they started to get ripe.
Makiinkweeminiiki, I say, pretending to
put berries in my mouth and
pointing down the trail
toward the bushes.
He nods his head.
Yes, he says,
blackberries. As we walk
to the berry patch, he tries my word—
makiinkweeminiiki, and I try his—*blackberries.*
I roll both words around like berries
in my mouth.

JAMES

Wonder if my mouth is purple-black, like Anikwa's. I start to head back
up the trail toward home. But wait—what's he saying? *Kiihkoneehsa*—

that means "fish"! He points to the river trail, meaning, *Follow me,* so I do.
When we get to the river, he pulls a string of seven fish out of the water

and gives me a nice-size trout. Wish I knew how he catches all these fish.
Thanks! I say, and then I repeat it in his language: *Neewe.* We walk along

together; I'm happy because he gave me this fish, so I start whistling.
He figures out the tune and whistles along with me. Yesterday, I found

a bee tree full of honey. Wonder if he's seen it. *C'mon,* I motion, *this way.*
It's off the trail a little, past the muddy place. We climb over the big log,

not far from where the trail splits, his trail going to Kekionga, and mine
going back to my house and the fort. Huh? What's that deep hole?

Looks like a person dug it. We step up for a closer look and jump back—
a man we've never seen before is standing in the hole, watching us!

ANIKWA

When I get home,
Grandma's cutting deer meat
into strips she's hanging on the drying rack.
I show her the fish I caught. She smiles.
Some for now, and some to salt
and save for winter.
We'll need more
salt before too long, she says.
Grandma, I say, *I saw a man.* She looks up.
Standing in a hole, I tell her, *near where the trail divides.*
He's not from here. Do you know who he is? She thinks about it.
I saw an Ojibwe man walking on that trail yesterday, she says. *Maybe*
he wants to see what's happening here. She doesn't seem scared.
She needs more hickory wood—her fire's almost out—
so I say, *Toontwa, let's get firewood for Grandma.*
Toontwa likes to eat—a lot—but he doesn't
like to carry firewood. *I saw foxes*
playing behind the big rock,
I tell him. *We could*
look for their den. That gets him
interested. *How many?* he asks. *Five,* I say.
I pick up my wood-carrying basket and walk off.
He follows with his basket like I
hoped he would.

JAMES

Ma asks, *What did you see today?* I tell her about a dead turtle in the creek, and a tree that fell across the trail, but I don't mention the man, or the hole

he must've dug. Ma might get worried and say I can't go out by myself. She's cutting up the fish when Pa comes in and sits down at the table.

Look what James brought home! she says. *Nice-looking trout,* says Pa. *Where did you catch it, Son?* I could pretend I caught it. But I know better than to

lie to Pa. That's one thing he won't abide. *Anikwa caught it,* I admit. Ma says, *Next time his aunt and uncle come to trade, give them a little extra.*

Ma calls Mink and Old Raccoon Anikwa's aunt and uncle, but Anikwa calls Old Raccoon his father. From what I can tell, Miami children

have a lot of parents. That's good if your ma and pa die, like his did. His mother died of smallpox when he was two years old, and then

a year later, his father got killed. *In a skirmish,* Pa said. *That's like a war, but smaller.* Makes me wonder: Who'd take care of me if Pa and Ma died?

ANIKWA

This lacrosse stick
is too big for me, but I like to use it
because it was my father's. Grandma tells me,
He was the best lacrosse player I ever saw.
He was so good, he could
make it seem like his
younger brother
was as good as he was.
I wish I remembered him better.
They say his voice was like strong music.
Everyone loved to listen to him speak. When people
started arguing, he said what he thought, and then stayed quiet
while other people spoke. People listened to him, and thought
carefully about anything he said. *His words,* Father says,
rose to the top, when we had to make hard decisions
about war or treaties—what to do
when all the changes came
across our land.
At first,
new kinds of sickness, then
a different kind of people—starting with men,
who soon brought families. Then soldiers, and the fort.
Like the bees that flew in from the east
and settled on our flowers.

JAMES

I'm going out fishing, alone, when here comes Isaac: *Where you going?* Dang.
I was hoping to catch a lot of fish and give one to Anikwa. I never see him

when Isaac's with me. Don't want to be mean, so I tell Isaac where I'm headed.
He walks along beside me, talking, talking, talking. *There's gonna be a war here.*

Not sure I'm supposed to tell you. Your pa and ma might not want you to know.
Like he's old enough to know about it, and I'm not—I'm older than he is!

Course I heard about it, I say, even though I haven't. I keep quiet, hoping
he'll say more, and he does: *My pa says the Indians are on the British side.*

That can't be true. *You don't know what you're talking about,* I blurt out.
They've been our friends since Ma was a girl. Her grandpa traded with them!

He shakes his head. *I know what I'm talking about, but you don't,* he says.
I bet you don't even know about the siege. I shrug, like I know but I don't care.

The Indians might block the fort, he says, *so we can't get out until the British come.*
Then they'll all join up and attack us. Trying to act like he knows everything.

ANIKWA

Kwaahkwa
and I came to this quiet
place to fish. We listen to the river
whisper in that soft, low voice
it has sometimes. There's
a pair of bluebirds
singing
on a low branch of the oak.
Two fish arc out of the water near
the eddy, showing us exactly where they are.
Then, over by that sycamore that fell last year, a big
bullfrog starts up talking like a drum. I answer, and he
answers back. And then we hear something else—
James's quiet voice, Isaac's scratchy loud one.
It sounds like they're arguing. Everything
except the river and the frog stops
talking. The bluebirds fly
away, the ducks dive
underwater.
We move into the shadows,
crouch down behind a rock, and watch.
Not exactly hiding, just staying quiet, listening
and keeping our eyes
open.

JAMES

Isaac keeps trying to show off how much he knows. *Don't worry, James,*
he says (he thinks I'm scared), *the Americans might get here first. Pa told me*

our army is bigger than the British army. But if the Indians join the British,
we're done for. He slices his hand across his throat. I know how to scare him:

lead him past the hole I saw when I was with Anikwa. If that man's still
standing in it, Isaac will jump out of his skin. Better not, though. He'd tell

his ma, and she'd tell mine, and they'd make us stay inside the stockade
where they could keep an eye on us. I'd hate that. We're walking by the river,

near where Anikwa gave me the fish, when Isaac comes to a sudden stop.
Look! He points. *Over there by that tree!* He picks up a rock and throws it

as hard as he can. *I think I hit it!* He runs over, leans down, and holds up
a dead bullfrog, so proud of himself. *Isaac,* I ask, *what'd you do that for?*

That frog didn't hurt you. He stares at me. *For fun,* he says. *How come you*
never like to have fun? I look around—I sure hope Anikwa isn't watching.

ANIKWA

Splash!
The frog stops talking.
Did it jump out of the way in time?
Did it sink down in the mud?
Or—did that rock hit it?
I lean back so I can
see: Isaac
lifts the bullfrog
from the water at the river's edge.
The frog's legs (strong enough to cross a creek
in two jumps) dangle from his hands. Isaac smiles like
he's in a war against the frogs and he just won a battle. I grab
a rock to throw at *him*, but Kwaahkwa says, *You know
frogs taste good. That boy gets hungry, just like us.*
Then Isaac swings the bullfrog by its legs,
around and around, over his head.
He's about to throw it
in the deep part
of the river.
No one will have that frog
for supper. I jump up and run to try
to stop him, or catch the frog, but it goes flying
through the air just before I
grab Isaac's arm.

JAMES

Isaac and Anikwa slip in the mud and end up in the river. I didn't see
which one pushed first, but they could both get pulled downriver.

Who should I help? I pick up a long branch and lie down on the bank
to hold it out. Isaac reaches it first—he grabs it and pulls himself up.

Anikwa is still in the water, sputtering from all the water in his nose
(and because he's mad about that frog, I bet). I don't see Kwaahkwa

coming until he reaches out to Anikwa, pulls him out of the water,
and starts talking fast—not sure what they're saying, but it looks

like Anikwa would push Isaac back in the river if Kwaahkwa didn't
stop him. Anikwa takes off his moccasins, squeezes out the water, and

puts them back on, glaring at Isaac the whole time. He walks away with
Kwaahkwa, glancing at the river where the dead frog floats downstream.

Isaac shakes himself like a dog trying to get dry. *See?* he says to me.
That boy just attacked me for no reason! I told you they're not on our side.

SALT'S LONG, SLOW JOURNEY

The earth lifts and tilts.
Water flows
from high ground
to low, around
and under rock.
Salt carried by water
moves through sand.
Salt and sand
through time,
pressed into stone.

ANIKWA

Seven raccoon,
one fox, four otter, sixteen beaver,
two deer. Their meat has fed us; now Father
counts the pelts he'll trade. Grandma has
a basket of maple sugar. Toontwa
has a rabbit skin and I have
two skunk pelts.
Mink made three extra
pairs of moccasins to trade. Now
we're ready. We start down the trail, talking
about what we need: a pair of socks, a ball of twine,
a new blade for the ax. A copper cooking pot. Needles, thread.
Cotton cloth. Red, blue, and yellow ribbons. *Salt?* asks Mink.
Father scowls and says, *When I was a boy, we walked*
to the salt licks, or our Shawnee friends brought
salt when they came to visit. I don't like
to buy it from the traders.
Mink is quiet.
We have to have salt—
without it, we get sick when we work
in the hot sun. But she understands. *We'll get salt*
next time, she says. A blackbird flies past.
Aya, niihka, I say. *Hello, friend.*

JAMES

Anikwa comes up the trail with his family. I haven't seen him since Isaac
killed the bullfrog—is he mad? At me? *Hello,* I say. He answers, *Aya . . . niihka.*

He names the pelts he's carrying. *Paapankamwa* (fox). *Amehkwa* (beaver).
And others—too many words to remember. I carry a basket for his grandma,

and she smiles and calls me *myaamiinse*—that means "Miami child." This basket
is full of maple sugar, and she always has a little extra. While they're trading,

Anikwa plays a tune on a willow whistle. Could I make one? I point to the whistle
and take out my knife. We go find a willow tree, and Anikwa shows me how

to cut a stick at an angle, make a notch through the bark, and tap the stick all over
so the bark comes loose and slips right off. After I slice off a piece of wood

to make a mouthpiece, he helps me cut another notch and slide the bark back on.
I put the whistle to my mouth and blow—it works! The sound it makes is lower

than Anikwa's. He plays fast, and I play slow; soft, loud, then soft again.
We sound so good, two yellow birds stop to listen and sing along with us.

ANIKWA

When we
walk into the trading post
playing our whistles, they've finished
with their trading. Grandma saved
some maple sugar, and gives
us each a big piece
(a tiny piece
for baby Molly). James's father
gives us each a stick of licorice candy—
it tastes like flowers and honey mixed together,
and I suck on mine as we start home. So does Toontwa.
But Rain Bird puts hers in her pocket without even tasting it!
She's never done that before. What's wrong with her?
Mink glances a quick question at Grandma,
who raises her eyebrows for a second
as they both look at my sister.
A quiet smile crosses
Rain Bird's face,
like a bird
landing on a branch,
then flying off again. I notice something
for the first time—some people might think Rain Bird
has a pretty face. This smile makes her
look older.

JAMES

Ma gives Molly a hard crust to chew—she has two new teeth, ready
to pop through. *Play with her, will you, James? She's so fussy, you're*

the only one who can make her smile. I let her pull my hair—she likes that,
but the trouble is, she's getting stronger and it hurts! I wiggle my toes

in the new moccasins Ma got for me today—she knits wool socks to trade
for moccasins Mink makes. They've done that all my life. Ma says to Pa,

The trading seemed fair today. He doesn't answer right away. *Yes,* he finally
says. Then: *The President and Governor have asked me to try to sell more goods*

to the Miami than they can afford, to deliberately get them into debt. Ma says,
We don't go into debt ourselves. It would be wrong to encourage others to do so.

Pa explains, *We'd get paid next time they sign a treaty. If they sell some*
of their land, the government will pay off their debt as part of the agreement.

At first it sounds fair, but then I think about it more. If they sell their land,
where will they hunt and pick berries and plant corn? Where will they live?

ANIKWA

I figured out why
Rain Bird hid her licorice candy.
We're all playing tossball when I notice
Kwaahkwa's mouth is stained black,
different from makiinkweemina
stains. Rain Bird gave
her licorice
to Kwaahkwa! Why would
she do that? I try to act like I don't
notice, but Toontwa sees it too, and he can't
swallow his laughter. I toss the ball to him to make him stop
laughing long enough to hold it up and decide where to toss it next.
Miililo, Kwaahkwa shouts. *Give it to me!* Toontwa forgets about
the licorice and throws the ball to Kwaahkwa—happy
because Kwaahkwa noticed him. Kwaahkwa's
happy too, because Rain Bird is watching
when he makes a goal—she
has that same smile
on her face.
When the game is over,
we gather round the fire to eat:
roasted raccoon, hot corn, beaver soup.
Fireflies light up the edge
of the dark forest.

JAMES

Wish Molly would hurry up and get big so she could help
find moss to plug the cracks between the logs. Gotta do it,

or the wind will blow right through our walls. Ma never stops
fretting about winter, even now when we're all sweating

in the summer sun. We've never yet frozen to death—I doubt
it will happen this year. But Ma handed me a sack and said,

See if you can fill it, so here I am, lifting moss from rocks, shaking
off the sticks and spiders. When I look up, a mother deer with two

fawns is watching me—one of them has a white patch on its leg.
Now here come two bucks. They all stand there together, trying

to make me lonesome. When they turn and walk away, I could follow
to see where they go. I could tell Pa where they are so he could go out

and get one. He'd be happy; the meat would taste good. But those little
ones . . . naw. My moss sack is full. I go home and help Ma stuff the cracks.

ANIKWA

We're down by the river,
cutting cattails to make walls for the longhouse.
Toontwa calls us over: *Look,* he says, *fresh tracks in the mud.*
One set of big tracks, two sets of small ones—
a mother black bear and her cubs
came here to drink, early
this morning,
and we don't want
to surprise them or disturb them.
Grandma speaks quietly, in case they're nearby:
We'll go home on the other trail, and come back later. We've
been here all afternoon, and now we spread the cattails in the sun.
We should have enough to sew together into three more mats,
to cover the frame we're working on. We've cut saplings,
dug holes to set them in the ground. Next, we'll tie
the frame together. We'll finish this longhouse
before the geese fly south. When it's cold,
the cattail walls will keep out
wind and snow.
Our fire will keep us warm
inside while we tell winter stories. Today,
these cattails spread out on the ground make me think
of winter. In winter, the longhouse will
remind me of this summer day.

JAMES

Isaac comes to the door. *Let's go do something.* Not sure I want to—
doing things with Isaac usually leads to trouble. But we head out,

walking by the river. He finds some cattails and whacks them on a tree
to make the brown parts burst. All the fluff goes flying—looks like fun.

Let me try that, I say. *Where'd you get those?* Then I see: cattail reeds are
laid out on the ground beside the long green leaves, drying in the sun.

Isaac grabs as many reeds as he can hold. *Leave them alone,* I say. *People
put these here—they'll be back to get them.* But Isaac never listens to me.

He keeps busting up the cattails' fluffy parts and walking on the reeds,
leaving muddy boot prints all over them. Then he stomps across all the

animal tracks so I can't see what animals have been here. *Hey, look!* he says,
pointing. *A hornet nest!* Before I can stop him, he whacks it with a stick—

the hornets come raging out, and we run off. I get stung six times! Isaac:
not once. I'm hollering in pain. He's laughing his head off—just like usual.

ANIKWA

Four men
went out looking for
the black bears—they followed
the tracks around a bend
in the river, then
farther, until,
two hours
from Kekionga, they saw
where the tracks crossed a shallow place
to the other side. Even though they didn't find the bears,
now we know it's safe to go back for our cattails. They should be
lighter, easier to carry home, after drying out here in the sun all day.
The weather's good: warm, but not too hot, no rain, not many
flies or mosquitoes. Black and orange butterflies
all around us, like flying flowers,
and others, deep purple-
blue, the color
of the
sky
on a half-moon night.
Here's where we left the cattails.
What? Who did this? Why are all these hornets
flying everywhere, so lost
and angry?

JAMES

What happened to your face? Ma asks. Don't want her to know about the cattails.
Hornet nest, I say—maybe that'll be enough. But she keeps asking questions

until she figures out what happened. Like I expect, she says, *You'll have to
go back and cut new cattails.* Then: *I'll go with you.* As we walk, Molly laughs

at the butterflies fluttering around her, the wind blowing through her hair.
Could've been a good time. No hornets—no Isaac. But when we get to where

the cattails are, Anikwa is already there with his family, studying the tracks
around the broken reeds. My moccasins and Isaac's boots—the same size.

They look at my feet. Do they notice that it's Isaac's muddy tracks, not mine,
that ruined all their cattails? Anikwa's grandma looks at me like she can

see my thoughts. She searches around, picks some plants, takes my face
in her hands, and presses leaves on all the hornet stings—cool on my hot skin.

I don't look at her. (Sometimes I'm glad she can't talk English.) I watch
to see what Anikwa does—then take out my knife and start cutting cattails.

SALT CRYSTALS SHINE

Sunlight travels
through the sky
as water flows
within the earth
dissolving salt,
carrying it on.

When salty water
surfaces to light,
salt crystals shine,
a jeweled ring
around this shallow
pool of brine.

ANIKWA

The longhouse
is finished. Now we're helping
Kwaahkwa's family put the roof on their log
house, and stuff the cracks with moss.
Soon it will be time to bring in
our corn and dry it
for the winter.
If we dry enough corn
and fish and meat; if snow doesn't
come too soon, or last too long; if no one
gets sick this year—maybe we will all survive until
next summer. Today lots of friends and relatives from
other villages are coming. We'll have games—
lacrosse and tossball—food and music,
stories, dancing. *Come on, Toontwa,*
let's get plenty of firewood,
so the fire will last
all night long.
This time,
he comes running,
glad to help, because he knows
the longer we keep the fire burning, the more
time we'll have with our friends
and cousins.

JAMES

I have my snares in my pocket, and I know exactly where to set them.
I'm heading out the door, when Ma says, *Wait a minute, James.* What?

She's always glad to see me snare some rabbits. She likes rabbit meat,
and she needs a few more skins to make a coat and hat for Molly.

She hesitates. *Maybe you should stay inside the stockade today,* she says.
But, Ma, I argue, *there's no rabbits inside the stockade!* She frowns.

Well, something's been eating my cabbages. See what you catch in my garden.
I tried that already. Everyone knows, rabbits like to stay on their trails.

Yesterday, one hopped down the river trail and looked right at me,
like a challenge. *I won't go far,* I say. *I promise!* She's thinking about it.

I'll pick some blackberries, I add. *All right,* she finally says. *But don't go
farther than the berry patch. And . . . let me know if you see anything unusual.*

I'm out the door, through the stockade gate, and halfway to the trail
before I stop to wonder what Ma means by "anything unusual."

ANIKWA

Kwaahkwa is our
best lacrosse player, but he sure
likes to tease the little kids. *Toontwa*, he says,
*you call that a stick? That little twig
with an acorn on the end?*
Toontwa is proud
of his stick.
He worked hard
on it, and I helped him.
What do you expect? I say. *He's only
six years old.* Toontwa stands beside me, trying
to make himself look bigger, and Kwaahkwa smiles.
Let me have a look, he says, reaching for the stick.
He tightens a few knots, and gives it back,
then tosses the ball to Toontwa, who
scoops it up and throws it back to
Kwaahkwa. Toontwa won't
play in the men's
game tonight,
but we're all having fun
before the big game starts. *Miililo!* I call,
holding up my stick. I get the ball and throw it toward
Toontwa. He runs for it and looks up to catch
Kwaahkwa's smile.

JAMES

Before I set my snares, I look for pawpaws. Should be almost ripe.
Yes—here's the tree I found last year. Even more fruit this year.

I go check the bluebird nest. Good—all four babies, still alive in there.
Five or six more days, they'll leave the nest—hope I get to see that.

I come to the oak tree that fell in the river, half in, half out of the water.
Ducks and geese swim past. A pair of herons lifts out of a treetop.

I sit on the dry end of the log, staying still so I don't scare the turtles
when they climb out on the log's other end: two . . . four . . . five . . . seven.

A family of raccoons was here this morning, Anikwa's tracks mixed in
with theirs. His tracks are like mine because Mink makes the same

kind of moccasins for him as she makes to trade with Ma. I follow his
tracks—going toward that hole we saw. Don't want to get too close,

so I climb a tree to look down into it. Empty. From up here, I can see
the berry bush. Anikwa's there, with Toontwa—do they see me up here?

ANIKWA

Aya, James calls out
as he climbs down from the tree.
He saw me before I had a chance to trick him
into thinking I'm a crow, but I make
a crow call on my whistle
anyway, and then I
show him
how to do it.
Looks like he's come out
to try to snare some rabbits. I point
to a pile of rabbit droppings in the middle of the trail.
Waapanswa, I say, and he repeats, *Waapanswa,* smiling because
he's learned another word. But then, not far down the trail,
he points to raccoon droppings and says, *Waapanswa.*
Now, that's funny. I put my hands on my head
to look like rabbit ears, and say again:
Waapanswa. James grins. *Oh,*
you mean "rabbit"!
He hops
down the trail to show he knows
what *waapanswa* means. We start laughing.
Then we look up and there's a man I've never seen before,
standing in the shadow of a tree,
watching us.

JAMES

Who is this man? If he was from Kekionga, Anikwa would know him, and
I would've seen him in the trading post. When he sees us looking at him,

he turns and walks away. I stand here with Anikwa and Toontwa—not
laughing anymore. We follow the trail to where it curves around the pond.

I pick up a flat stone and toss it. *One, two, three . . . four skips!* I say, holding
up four fingers. Anikwa finds a stone and throws it, holding up one finger

for each skip. His stone sinks after three skips, but he holds up four fingers.
I shake my head: *No, three!* I say, holding up three fingers. He doesn't

argue back; he picks up another stone and skips it five times—good ones, too,
you can see the ripples from each bounce. I try again, but I can't get past four.

We head down the river trail. I set my last snare. Then Toontwa and Anikwa
walk toward Kekionga, and I head home, thinking about that man we saw.

Is this what Ma means by "unusual"? Naw. I have to come back tomorrow
to check my snares. What's so unusual about someone standing by a tree?

ANIKWA

The person we saw
behind the tree has come to Kekionga. He's
an Ottawa man, named Wedaase. We've eaten together,
and now we're sitting by the fire playing music.
Father on his fiddle, Wedaase on a flute,
Kwaahkwa with the drummers.
Rain Bird and her friends
start dancing, and later, when the music
ends, Kwaahkwa's father starts a conversation:
This war that's coming could make those other wars look easy.
The Americans are marching from the east, the British from the north—
from what I hear, they're in Detroit right now. The two armies could be here soon,
fighting each other—for our land. Father looks serious. Wedaase goes on,
The British will give guns and ammunition to anyone who helps
fight the Americans. A lot of warriors, from many places,
plan to join the British because after we defeat
the Americans, the British will leave this
part of the country for all the tribes
to share. Would there be
room here—for everyone? If the British win,
won't they want to live here, too? No matter who wins,
the soldiers will be hungry when they're fighting. They'll take our food.
Grandma must be thinking the same thing. *We should hide*
our dried meat and corn, she says.

JAMES

Isaac's ma comes to our house with Mrs. Graves and Mrs. Carlson.
Ma invites them in but gives them the same look she's been giving Pa,

meaning, *Don't talk about it in front of the children.* They lower their voices.
I go to the washbasin and act like I don't even know they're here,

scrubbing a spot of pine pitch off the back of my hand. Isaac's ma says,
For heaven's sake, Lydia, move into the fort until this is over. The stockade

might protect you from wild animals, but you need soldiers to protect you
from— Ma interrupts: *We will stay in our own home. I have never been*

afraid of any of our neighbors. I glance at the provisions we've stored up
for the winter. If there is a siege like Isaac said, how long will they last?

Mrs. Briggs spits out her next words: *You're brave now, but how brave*
will you be when your house is burning? What if they capture James or Molly?

Ma picks Molly up and squeezes her, like she does when she gets mad
at me or Pa. But this time, it's her lady friends she pushes out the door.

DEER COME TO THE SALT

Heart-shaped
tracks in soft mud
point to salty places
where deer come to lick
the earth. Something here
they need, something
they like. Heads down,
they lick and lick this
place that tastes
so good to them.

ANIKWA

Last winter
an ice storm coated each branch
of the trees by the river trail. Rain started
one evening and froze in the night,
bending tall trees to the ground.
Some branches broke—
they hang high
in the trees—and now the wind
is rising. I'm walking with Kwaahkwa,
not far from home. We hear a branch crash down.
Dangerous-sounding. Where is it? Then a sharp cry:
Watch out! A boy's voice—is it James? Who's with him?
He might be hunting deer with his father, or maybe
checking his snares. We walk toward the sound,
staying hidden, watching what lies ahead.
Over there—yes, it is James—Isaac
is with him, crying, his leg
pinned under a branch.
That boy is mean.
We don't like him. But we can't
leave them out here alone. I call out, *Aya, niihka.*
James answers, *Aya, Anikwa!* Isaac looks scared. Of us?
Don't worry, James says to him, *"Aya, niihka"*
means "Hello, friend."

JAMES

I've never been so glad to see Anikwa. Isaac is crying. I can't lift the branch.
I don't have a saw to cut it. Maybe Anikwa and Kwaahkwa can help us.

But what does Isaac do? He stops crying, pulls his knife out of its sheath,
holds it up, and starts yelling, *Stay away! I'm warning you!* I grab the knife

out of his hand. *What are you doing?* I ask him. Kwaahkwa and Anikwa
stop, step back, and watch. I can't make Isaac stop talking. He whispers,

too loud, *My ma and pa warned me not to talk to Indians. What if they try to
capture us?* He struggles to lift the branch, gives up, and cries out in pain.

His pants are ripped, there's a bruise on his leg, a bloody scratch on his face.
Isaac, I say, *it will take too long to go to the fort for help. We're closer to Kekionga.*

These friends could help us lift the branch. From the look on his face, you'd think
I told him to crawl right into a bear's den. *Listen to me,* I beg, *don't act like this.*

I can't lift the branch by myself. And I can't leave you here all alone. He sniffles.
All right, he finally agrees. But when I look up, Anikwa and Kwaahkwa are gone.

ANIKWA

What would
he do if we got close enough
to help him? What will happen if we
leave them alone out here?
All the way back
to Kekionga
we talk
about what to do.
Leave him there, Kwaahkwa argues.
He deserves whatever happens. I'm not going back—
let him protect himself with his puny maalhseenhsi. I can't help
laughing about how Isaac waved that knife around like he thought
we were dangerous. *Let's sneak up behind him and growl,*
I say. Kwaahkwa laughs. I growl at him,
and he pretends to be scared.
We're almost home—
who's behind us?
James calls out,
Aya, niihka.
I look at Kwaahkwa. We stop
and wait for James to catch up. He points
and motions for us to follow him back to Isaac, but Kwaahkwa
points to Kekionga. *Moohci,* he says. *No.*
You follow us.

JAMES

Kekionga smells good: smoke rising up from the houses, deer meat
roasting . . . and something else, maybe hot corn? Makes me hungry!

Old Raccoon comes out to meet us, and Kwaahkwa starts talking,
pointing—must be telling him what happened. Old Raccoon looks at me

long and hard. *I'll take you home,* he says. (But . . . Isaac? We can't leave
him stuck under that branch!) Old Raccoon says something that makes

Kwaahkwa mad. Then he switches to English and tells me, *They'll stay
with your friend. We'll go get help.* Wiinicia gives us each a handful

of corn, still warm, and a piece of hot deer meat. Anikwa and Kwaahkwa
start down the trail while Old Raccoon gets his horse. He boosts me up on it

and gets on behind me. We ride fast, but he takes the long trail that doesn't
go past the fort—maybe he doesn't want any soldiers to see us. He stops

outside the trading post. I get Pa, and explain everything as fast as I can.
Thank y— Pa starts to say, but Old Raccoon has already turned to go home.

ANIKWA

We have our
bows and arrows. If we see
a wolf or bobcat come close to Isaac, we know
what to do. Otherwise, we won't
go near him. Does he even
know we're here?
We stand
in the shadows watching.
Doesn't he know he shouldn't cry
like that when he's out in the forest, hurt?
We have to stay here and make sure nothing happens
until James brings someone to help. I wish Isaac would keep
quiet—if the animals hear him, they'll know he's
injured. What's that in the trees, moving
toward him? Coming closer—bobcat!
Big one. Kwaahkwa aims
and his arrow flies
straight past
Isaac,
hitting the bobcat
right above the eyes. It takes
a few steps back, then drops to the ground.
Isaac whips his head around—
what just happened?

JAMES

I tell Ma exactly where Isaac is. Then Pa grabs his saw, and we ride out
to Isaac, while Ma takes Molly and runs to the fort for his parents.

We bring a blanket, a clean white cloth for a bandage, a bottle of water.
When we reach him, Isaac's face is streaked with dirt and tears, and he's

gasping: *They tried to shoot me! I saw them!* He's pointing at Kwaahkwa
and Anikwa, as they walk slowly into the woods. *Watch out,* Isaac yells,

they have bows and arrows! Bows at their sides, arrows on their backs.
Isaac—be quiet, I say. While Pa tries to calm him, I walk to meet Anikwa

and Kwaahkwa. They circle away from Isaac, into the forest behind him,
and Kwaahkwa pulls an arrow out of a dead bobcat's head. I piece together

the story, and go back to tell Isaac. *No,* he insists, *that big boy shot at me
and he missed!* Pa shakes his head. *Never mind,* he says. *Help me saw through*

this branch. Easy now. Isaac's parents arrive. *What happened?* they ask.
Isaac has a whole different story from mine—and they only listen to his.

THIS GAZE, THESE DEEP BROWN EYES

People follow deer
through the forest,
watching where they lick the ground.

The people scrape salt
into their hands, their baskets. They taste
the salt, bring it home.

Again and again, does and bucks and fawns,
porcupines and people,
meet at the salt place.

ANIKWA

Wedaase has been
to his home and back. He's talked
to Shawnee, Potawatomi, Wyandot, and Ojibwe people,
and come to sit with us beside our fire again.
Father has said many times, *We'll do all*
we can to keep this war away
from our home.
But Wedaase speaks six languages.
He has come a long distance, and everyone
listens with respect. *Brothers and sisters,* he says, *it's time*
for us to choose sides. The Americans won't stop until we stop them.
They're determined to have all the land. Yours, ours—everyone's. That much
is clear to anyone with eyes. If we join the British, and they help us win,
all our nations could live together on the land we still have.
Father is quiet for a long time. He looks around
the fire at everyone, sweeps his gaze
across the sky, over the trees,
to three cardinals,
bright red
against the sycamore's white bark.
A chipmunk pokes its head up from a hole beside
a maple tree. Father rests his eyes on me. *We want our children's*
children's children, he says quietly, *to grow old*
in their own home.

JAMES

Is that cranes I hear? It makes no sense—it's the middle of the morning,
and it sounds like five or six of them. They usually fly in at sunset.

I watch the sky for a long time and I don't see any cranes come in,
but there it is again, same sound. Maybe Anikwa, mimicking again?

I climb a tree near the stockade gate and look around. Yes, there he is,
hands to his mouth, making crane calls. I play a blackbird song on my

whistle, and he looks up, like he's trying to see if there are blackbirds
in this tree. When he sees me up here, I wave to him, jump down

and head for the gate to go say, *Aya*. But then Pa calls: *James, I need your
help in the trading post.* Strange thing, though—when I go to help him,

he can't think of anything for me to do. No one's here to trade. The floor
is clean. No spiderwebs to sweep away. Pa sees the question on my face

and says, *I might get busy a little later on. Stay around in case I need you.*
He wants me to stay inside the stockade, but he doesn't want to say so.

ANIKWA

Toontwa
heard it, too—not
blackbirds, exactly, but someone
trying to sound like them.
I told him it was James,
and then we saw
James
wave his hand—he
was coming down to see us.
But he just disappeared—we didn't
hear him whistling like blackbirds anymore;
he didn't come out through the stockade gate, or
through the place we know, where a board
is loose, and he can push it back
and squeeze through. Some
people are saying we
should stay away
from here.
Mink
heard someone say
they might close the trading post.
She thinks we should get everything we need
while we still can. *Come on, Toontwa,*
let's go home, I say.

JAMES

Ma's face is like the sky on a day the weather changes. Smiling like the sun came out, because she received a parcel from her family in Philadelphia.

Crying when she reads that her sister's baby, Lucy, only lived for seven days. Aunt Amanda made a quilt for Lucy, and she's giving it to Ma for Molly.

Ma says it's the color of the ocean she remembers from before she came here, when she was seventeen. *I hear the seagulls crying when I look at it,* she says.

I hold up the quilt for Ma to step back and admire. She lays it down, sets Molly on it—we smile when Molly tries to pick one of the stitched-on flowers.

Pa comes in and eats his lunch without saying anything to Ma or me. Something's wrong. Finally, he puts down his mug, looks up at Ma,

and tells her, *The soldiers are worried. They've asked me to stop selling essential provisions to anyone outside the fort.* A hundred questions fly across Ma's face,

but she doesn't ask them. *Just in case,* Pa adds. Ma looks out the window, silent. Just in case—what? In case Isaac's right, and there's a siege. Starting when?

ANIKWA

Mink

lays a pack of beaver pelts across

Rain Bird's arms and gives the berry basket to Toontwa.

Grandma says, *Remember, we need wiihkapaakani.*

Do you know what they call it?

Father scowls.

"*Salt*,"

he says. *They take it*

from our land, then sell it back to us.

He needs a beaver trap, ammunition for his rifle.

When we start off down the river trail, the sky is streaked

bright orange-red above the water. We'll have rain sometime today.

I tell Father where I saw a pair of coyotes, but he barely listens.

His steps are long, and I run to keep up. (He's been angry

ever since Grandma mentioned salt.) A hard

rain starts to fall just as we arrive

at the trading post. We walk in

and lay our furs out

on the counter.

Aya, Father says. James smiles.

Mr. Gray says, *Hello.* But he's looking at the floor.

He isn't smiling, and he doesn't touch the furs. James looks

back and forth from his father to mine,

to Toontwa, to me.

JAMES

Old Raccoon says, *We need salt,* and I reach for the salt scoop,
but Pa's next words slap my hand out of the air as fast as if he'd

reached out and grabbed it: *No more salt,* he says to Old Raccoon.
Pa is lying? Even Toontwa is tall enough to see that the salt barrel

is more than halfway full. Old Raccoon stares right down into it.
When he looks back up at Pa, it's a short glance. He doesn't smile.

Mink doesn't give me maple sugar, or call me *myaamiinse.*
They pick up their furs and walk straight out the door. Anikwa

glances at the jar of licorice sticks, but not at me, as they walk out,
and he and his whole family start down the trail toward Kekionga.

After they leave, I can't look at Pa. I've never heard him lie before.
Then he says, *No need to tell your mother about that.* So—he knows

Ma wouldn't like this. *We'll need this salt,* he says. Who does Pa mean
by "we"? Our family couldn't use this much salt in a hundred years.

ANIKWA

Father
walks fast when he's mad,
stepping over a fallen log like it's a stick.
I climb up on the log, jump down,
half run, trying to keep up.
He slows down some,
walks like each step
is a drumbeat. Two ducks fly by.
He aims his rifle, lowers it. *Better not waste*
my ammunition, he says. *I might need it for something*
bigger. After a while, I ask, *Why don't we go get our own salt?*
You could show Toontwa and me where to find it. Father doesn't answer
right away. He walks beside me in the rain, searching for words.
Every treaty says the same thing, he begins. *They* give us
permission *to use our land like we always have—*
"as long as the grasses grow and rivers flow."
We still have the right to use our trails.
We know where the salt licks are.
But now it's dangerous
for us to travel in our own country.
The new settlers don't know our trails, or where
we're going, or why. He stands still, watching the river.
Does it look to you, he asks, *like siipiiwi*
has stopped flowing?

THE DEER'S HEART

At
the salt lick,
an arrow hits its target.
    The heart of the deer
        stops beating. The deer falls.
    Blood slows in its veins,
muscle-bound or flowing
onto salt-crusted
earth.

JAMES

Six soldiers walk into the trading post. *We've come to move provisions
to the fort*, says Mr. Briggs. Pa helps carry the salt barrel to their wagon.

They're taking everything: rifles, ammunition, pots and pans, traps,
spoons, ladles, cloth, nails, needles, licorice, flour, oatmeal, beans, boots.

What's going on? I ask. *They want us to close the trading post*, Pa answers,
for a week or so. Isaac came in with the soldiers—I thought he came to see

me. Turns out he's here to help. *James*, he says, *give me a hand with this
bag of oats.* We lift it and carry it outside. It's raining, but the soldiers

aren't complaining, so I don't either. One of them—his name is Rupert—
lifts a big bag of flour and tosses it in the wagon like it's no weight at all.

I act like I know all about this, but when Isaac whispers, *Did you hear?*
I don't answer. *The siege is about to start*, he says. *Hundreds of Indians*

*are coming to Kekionga. We have to stay inside the fort until the army gets here.
No one knows how long it will last. Could be a few days—or it might be weeks.*

ANIKWA

It's raining.
Like everyone in Kekionga,
we've invited people we don't know
to stay with us. The man we saw
standing in the hole is here.
He's Ojibwe—Father
remembers him
from the Greenville treaty-signing,
and tells us the man's name means "Brings In Light."
It's true—light from the fire bounces off his face and shines on us.
Wedaase is here, too, sitting beside Father, telling everyone about the time
he saw me with James. He asks if I'm a spy for the Americans. (Does he mean it?)
My face turns hot, and Father answers for me: *We trust James and his family.*
His mother has always been kind to us. She took care of Anikwa's mother
when we were too sick to care for her ourselves. Ever since, we've
called her Sister. James is like a cousin to our children.
Wedaase says, *Be careful, friend. That kind*
of cousin can turn his back on you
when you need him most.
Father looks at Wedaase, then at me.
Is he remembering the kindness Mrs. Gray showed
my mother long ago, or is he thinking about the other day,
when Mr. Gray looked at the floor and said,
No more salt?

JAMES

Oatmeal for lunch again? Two raisins each for me and Ma, three for Pa.
Same as we had for lunch and breakfast yesterday! I'm sick of oatmeal.

Why can't we have bread and cheese for lunch? I ask. Ma looks at Pa. *Don't
complain,* he says. (I didn't complain—I only asked.) *We have to make*

our provisions last. (For how long?) He's already told me we can't go out
hunting or fishing "until this is over with." I look at my feet, and Molly's,

thinking about the moccasins Mink makes, and the socks Ma knits
for our Miami friends. Not just trading, more like friends or relatives.

Ma's being quiet. Could I talk to Pa about what Isaac said? *Pa,* I say,
Isaac says the Indians are on the British side. I thought they were on ours.

He answers: *They're coming here from all around—we don't know them all.
It's hard to say who our friends are.* Ma looks out the doorway. Dark clouds

are gathering behind the flag. *As long as we have no evidence to the contrary,*
she says, *we'll continue to treat the Miami as the friends they've always been.*

ANIKWA

The corn is almost ripe,
but not quite ready to be picked. Still,
we're picking it, working together from dawn to dark.
We don't know how much time we have, says Grandma.
We hope the corn will be dry enough to bury
so we can keep it out of sight,
away from soldiers.
My job is to dig deep holes
in places we hope no one will look, while
Rain Bird braids the husks together and hangs the corn
up to dry. I work harder than I ever have, ignoring the blisters
on my hands as I keep digging. Harder, faster. At first, Kwaahkwa helped.
Now he spends all his time with the young men, who argue: *We have to*
be ready when it happens. Cleaning rifles, making arrowheads,
bullets. *There will be more soldiers than we've ever seen.*
Even if the British get here first, we don't know
how much ammunition they will bring.
Grandma stands behind me,
her hands on my head
pressing gently, as if she could
keep me from growing. Doing what she can
to give me strength and courage. *I've always hoped,* she says,
that you would not become a man
in a time of war.

JAMES

Mrs. Briggs begs Ma, *Come with us! You'll be the only woman left behind.*
Think about your children! What if— Ma cuts her off: *I will stay in my home.*

Ma can sure be stubborn. All the women and children in the fort are going
to Piqua, Ohio, so they won't be here when the war starts. (Everyone stopped

saying "if the war starts." Now they're saying "when.") Isaac gets an idea.
James, he says, *you could come with us, even if your ma won't go.* Ma stares

at him and doesn't say no right away—is she thinking of sending me,
without her or Pa? She'd keep Molly here, and I'd go to Piqua by myself?

Isaac acts like she said yes. *It'll be more fun with you along. We get to camp*
out by a lake—they say there's some big walleyes in it. Like this is a fishing trip

where nothing could go wrong. I step back, away from Isaac. Mrs. Briggs
keeps arguing, *We'll have five soldiers to protect us.* Ma firmly answers, *No.*

Armed soldiers might make the trip more dangerous. Mrs. Briggs says, *We're*
trying to find two Indian guides to go with us. Would anyone do that for them?

ANIKWA

Father
and Mink and Grandma
are still trying to find a way to stop this war,
or to keep it away from our home.
But everyone knows it's
coming. Father
has to make
a hard decision. He tells us,
All the women and children are leaving the fort,
going to Piqua. They've asked us for guides to protect them.
A few people laugh at this. Father holds up his hand. *Some of these*
people are our friends and relatives. They will be safer if we offer our help.
We know, better than they do—they're unlikely to survive without us.
All these may be good reasons to help them, but none
are good enough. It sounds like he's decided
not to go, and not to ask anyone else
to make this dangerous trip.
There is one more thing
to think about,
he says. *Maybe if we help*
them, the Americans will see that we are not
their enemies. If we do this, will they help us keep peace here?
Piyeeto, our Shawnee friend, speaks up: *I will go.*
And Father says, *So will I.*

JAMES

Last week, this would have been ordinary food. Now it looks like a feast:
corn bread, cheese, hard-boiled eggs—a basket of food Ma's sending with

the people going to Piqua. When my stomach growls, she says, *They'll need it
more than we do.* Isaac's trying to act like he's glad to be going, but he keeps

chewing on his lip—he can't stop it from quivering. He gets on the horse,
trying hard to smile, and Mr. Briggs lifts Becca up in front of him. *Take care*

of your ma and sister, Son, he says. How does he expect Isaac to do that?
Everyone knows how many dangerous things could happen on this trip.

Ma taps Pa on his arm and nods toward the front of the line. Old Raccoon?
He's going along? And someone else at the back. *Who's that?* I ask.

Pa answers, *A Shawnee named Piyeeto who knows the trails and language
where they're going.* As Old Raccoon starts down the trail, Pa rests his hand

on my shoulder, and we watch until the last horse disappears around the bend
into the forest. Then Pa goes to the fort, and I walk home with Ma and Molly.

THE DEER'S LIFE AND OUR LIFE

Sun lit its path
and warmed it.
Earth gave it food.
Rain quenched its thirst.
Salt kept it strong.

Now its life will be ours:
food, strength, warmth.
We give thanks
for earth, rain, sun.
For salt. For deer.

ANIKWA

We light
a fire. We will keep it burning
until Father and Piyeeto return home.
Kwaahkwa stands in the circle
of the fire's light, holding
a bowl of soup,
and he shines
like a grown man.
He has joined the other men,
from here and other places, as they prepare
to run back and forth past the fort all day and night,
keeping all the soldiers inside until the British army arrives.
When the soldiers in the fort look out and see all our men
running, and hear them singing all night and all day,
we hope they will think there are more warriors
than there really are, and they will be afraid
to leave the fort. This is what we
have heard them call
a "siege."
I'm glad to know
the children and their mothers
are not there—James and Mrs. Gray
and baby Molly should be
at Piqua now.

JAMES

I follow a raindrop down the window with my finger. When it gets to the bottom,
I find another one to follow. Nothing to do. Even if there was—no one to do it with.

I'm hungry! There's a squirrel up in that tree, looking right at me. I could get it
with my slingshot—easy. Or I could set a snare and catch a rabbit. Maybe two.

This time tomorrow we could be eating fried rabbit instead of soggy oatmeal.
Pa told us what's about to happen—maybe tomorrow, next day at the latest—

the fort will be surrounded by a lot of Indians we don't know, all of them hoping
the Americans won't get here in time, and we'll surrender when the British come.

But the way I see it—that hasn't happened yet. This might be my last chance to slip
out for a few minutes. Pa's at the fort, like he is every afternoon. Pretty soon,

Molly will take a nap. Usually Ma falls asleep when Molly does, long enough
for me to run a little ways along the trail, set my snares, and still get back

before she wakes up. The rain is slowing down, almost stopped. I slip three snares
into my pocket. Molly's yawning. So is Ma. They both close their eyes. Here I go.

ANIKWA

What's this?

It looks like James's snare.

He must have set it before he went to Piqua,

so he doesn't know he caught a rabbit.

Father and Piyeeto will be back

in a few days, but the women

and children will stay

a while longer. What should I do?

This rabbit was just caught—it's still warm.

I'd better take it out before a hungry paapankamwa

comes along, flashing his bushy red tail, showing off those

big sharp teeth. I'd give this rabbit to James's father if I could,

but since the trading post is closed, I'll have to take it home.

Here's another snare—looks like I got here too late—only

a tuft of brown fur, left over from paapankamwa's

rabbit feast. There might be another one

probably not far along the trail.

I know where to look.

Here it is,

empty, like the last one.

Paapankamwa must be hungry.

I'll leave the empty snares where I found them

for James to find when he

comes back.

JAMES

My mouth is watering for rabbit meat. My stomach's growling again. *Go check your snares,* it says. *Hurry, before a fox finds them.* Drowning out Ma and Pa's

warnings. They don't know I went out yesterday—lucky for me. Pa is over at the fort again. Molly's fast asleep, and Ma's eyes are closing. If I go

soon and come straight home, they won't even know I've left till I get back, and I won't tell them unless I have a rabbit for our supper. Like yesterday—

open the door, slip out, close it. (Glad there's no ladies around to spy on me.) I run to the loose board, push through, and take the path around the pond.

A beaver slaps his tail and dives. I don't wait to see where he comes up. I watch the trail ahead, look all around—don't see anyone. Here's my first

snare. Dang! Empty except for a piece of rabbit fluff. Something got to it before I did—probably a fox. Shoot! Second one's empty, too. That fox family

is having a feast. I should put out fox traps so they get caught before they steal my rabbits. One more snare to check. Gotta get home before Ma wakes up.

ANIKWA

I'm walking
along, thinking about
something Wedaase said last night:
We would all be better off if we
kept explorers, soldiers,
traders, settlers, and
missionaries
far away from here. If we can't
push them back behind the mountains, we can
at least try to keep them on the other side of the Ohio River.
What would our life be like without any of those people? Do we
need the trading post? Wedaase says, *Our grandparents got along fine*
without trade goods, not so long ago, and we could do it again now.
Maybe we have all the cooking pots we need. How about
rifles? Needles. Cloth. Could we make our clothes
like old-time people used to? We don't need
their food. I'd be happy if I never
saw Isaac again. I might
miss James.
(He'd miss me more.)
I wonder how he's doing at Piqua. Father
should be back soon. What? Who's that on the trail?
It looks like James . . . walking
right toward me!

JAMES

Hey! There's Anikwa, walking off with my rabbit! I thought
it was a fox that got them. But now I see what really happened—

Anikwa stole them! So it's true, what Pa said—sometimes it's hard
to say who our friends are. Looks like Anikwa turned into my enemy!

Well, if that's what happened, I know how to get my rabbit back.
I raise my arm to punch Anikwa. He drops the rabbit, grabs my arm,

stares at me like I'm a stranger. We've never fought before—I've always
thought I'd beat him if we did, but now I'm not so sure. He shoves me

and I fall in the mud. (Dang. Ma will find out everything.) Anikwa says
something I don't understand. "Papa come on?" Why can't he talk English?

He turns toward the rabbit, but I grab his foot so he falls in the mud, and he
can't reach it. I'm so hungry, I can taste that rabbit! I hold Anikwa down

with one arm and grab the rabbit with the other. Then I get up and run.
When I stop and look back, Anikwa is standing on the trail. Watching me.

ANIKWA

He thinks
I stole that waapanswa
from his snare! I tried to tell him, *It was
paapankamwa, not me!* But I couldn't
think of his word while he was
trying to punch me!
(Is it "fox"?)
Why can't he speak
our language? He's lived here
all his life, he should have learned by now.
Maybe it's true, what Wedaase said: *That kind of cousin
can turn his back on you.* Now I wish James *had* gone to Piqua.
He didn't hurt me any. I could have pushed him harder if I
wanted to. That crow flew up into a tree and now he's
laughing at me. I say, *You might taste just as good
as waapanswa.* He stops laughing, flies ahead
of me all the way home. Seems like
he wants to keep laughing,
but instead he's
saying, *James, ha ha, James.*
Calling me names and teasing me for
getting pushed in the mud by a mihši-maalhseensa.
Wedaase is right—we don't need
any of them.

JAMES

I stop at the pond and wash up—better to go home wet than muddy.
Anikwa never stole from me before. I would've given him a rabbit if

I got more than one. Why did he go and steal one before I had a chance?
Look at that beaver carrying branches into its house for winter food.

Most years, about this time, we're storing food for winter, too. Butchering pigs,
making bacon, picking up nuts, drying apples. This year, we just hope

we kept enough provisions for ourselves, to last until the siege is over.
What if we run out, and can't get any more? Will Ma change her mind

and move into the fort? If we're starving, she'll have to. Won't she?
Is there enough food in the fort for everyone? What's that—I hear someone

laughing—the kind of laugh where you try not to make a sound but you can't
help it. There's someone behind that bush, three Indians I've never seen before—

not from Kekionga—crouching down, trying to hide. I walk slowly past,
pretending I don't know they're there. Then I start walking faster. Then I run.

ANIKWA

Kwaahkwa
got another deer today,
and we're cooking a big pot of soup
because a lot of people will eat
with us tonight. More and
more people arrive
every day.
Potawatomi, Delaware,
Ottawa, Ojibwe, Kickapoo, Peoria,
Shawnee, and Miami. All the warriors agree,
we have to be ready to fight on the side of the British
when they get here. But Grandma and the other elders are still
trying to keep the war away from Kekionga. They've seen
what happens when there's fighting on our land.
Grandma says, *We barely have enough food*
to last us through a mild winter—
if war comes, the soldiers
will take our food.
Maybe burn
our houses. How can we
survive all that again? It scares me. My
grandfather, father, and uncle were all killed in battle.
Kwaahkwa is ready to fight. And Father
will fight if he has to.

JAMES

Ma meets me at the door: *Where have you been?* I drop the rabbit at her feet.
She looks me up and down, sees I'm soaking wet. And mad. Her face says

three things at once: *We told you to stay inside the stockade. Get in here
right now and change into dry clothes.* But also: *James, you got a rabbit!*

She puts Molly down and picks it up. *Should've been three of 'em,* I say.
Anikwa must have got there first. Two rabbits hop across my mind—

but before I have a chance to think about them, Ma starts asking a hundred
questions, and, like usual, I end up telling her too much. Pa comes home,

smells the rabbit cooking, asks Ma where it came from—and she tells him
everything, including (wish I hadn't told her) about the men I heard laughing.

When he hears that, Pa gets serious. *James,* he says, *look at me.* I look at him.
I thought you understood this: you are to stay inside the stockade at all times.

Then, in that same voice, *Lydia, we have to move into the fort until we see
what's going to happen.* Ma looks like she's about to cry, but she agrees.

ANIKWA

Kwaahkwa
teases me: *I heard you had*
a fight with your friend James this afternoon.
Three men saw the whole thing and
now they're telling everyone
that I'm a better
fisherman
than fighter. *I wasn't*
trying to win a fight, I say. *I was trying*
to make him see that I'm no thief! Grandma looks up
from the deerskin she's scraping. *I thought all the children*
over there went to Piqua with their mothers, she says. *But if James*
and the baby and their mother are still here—we have to find out
if they're still in their house. It's right inside the stockade.
Mink and Rain Bird both look worried. Why?
It's easier to burn down houses of people
you don't know, says Rain Bird.
That's how I figure out
what's going on:
someone is planning
to set the stockade on fire! When?
What if they burn down James's house?
Is anyone thinking of a way
to warn them?

VEINS LIKE RIVERS

The hunter lifts the deer,
holds the weight
of muscle, bone, and skin
as blood flows
through his own veins like rivers,
and sweat moves
through his skin, leaving,
when it dries,
a layer of translucent
crystals—salt.

JAMES

Ma folds our clothes and puts them in her trunk. *Here's the first pair
of moccasins Mink ever made for you,* she says. They'd fit Molly now.

I put my finger through a hole I wore through the deerskin when I
first learned to walk. Under this pair is another pair, a little bigger;

under them, another—nine pairs, right up to the size I'm wearing now.
One time Pa got me a pair of boots, but I hated how they pinched my feet.

When Mink makes moccasins, she sews the seams on top so they're
soft and comfortable, and I can run fast when I'm wearing them.

Ma puts the moccasins on top of the trunk, covers them with the quilt
from Aunt Amanda, closes the lid, and looks up. *I'm ready,* she says.

Pa has a wagon right outside the house. When I go out to help load it up,
I hear spring peepers on the other side of the stockade. Makes no sense—

it isn't spring, and we're not close to water. It can only mean one thing:
Anikwa is close by, trying to get my attention. Wonder what he wants.

ANIKWA

I can see
through the stockade gate:
The trading post is empty. It looks like
James and his family are moving
out of their house,
into the fort.
A soldier
is outside in a field,
feeding the cows and pigs, taking
eggs from those birds they call "chickens."
Why do they keep their animals penned in like that,
so they have to feed them every day? They could let them loose
to get their own food. Wedaase and Father argued about that.
They hunt our animals, everywhere they go, Wedaase said.
We should take theirs to replace them. Father answered,
They have their ways, we have ours. We've lived
with these people for a long time.
Some of them are friendly.
A few are relatives.
Don't give the Americans a reason
to attack us when they get here. Wedaase said,
Do you think they'll need a reason? There's only one way
to keep them out: attack them first, harder
than they attack us.

JAMES

Now I see why we're adding water to bean soup that's already thin,
and why we're almost out of oatmeal. There's eighty men in this fort,

with hardly any food. We brought what we had to share but it wasn't
enough, even for our family—it's like nothing for all these hungry men.

A soldier named Patrick comes in carrying a basket: eighteen eggs,
an onion, and seven potatoes. That's what we all have for supper.

Pa says, *We'll manage. Let's hope the hens keep laying. We can always kill
the cows and pig. We'll be able to last a week—as long as the stockade holds.*

Ma puts a blanket on the floor for me, and I lie down, but I can't sleep.
I keep thinking about what Pa said: *a week? as long as the stockade holds?*

The soldiers are saying the British have cannons that could knock a hole
in the stockade. I think about that as I fall asleep, and a picture comes to

me: a hole, rabbits running out of it, jumping through a hoop of fire. Fire . . .
Guns can't protect us against fire. And rabbits . . . I just thought of something.

ANIKWA

Father is home!
We go to the longhouse to hear
what he and Piyeeto have seen and heard.
We got them all to Piqua, Father says,
and took some time to look around.
The Americans have several
thousand soldiers.
About as many more are coming
from Kentucky—then they'll march this way.
They could be here within a week. Mink and Grandma
listen quietly. Later, I stay awake to hear them talk. *If the men*
decide to go ahead with what they're planning, Mink says, *everything*
will change after tonight. Grandma doesn't answer for a long time.
Then she says: *We can't stop things from changing. I hope*
the children will remember how our life has been.
Moonlight shines through an opening
in the door. A mouse scuffles
around in the fire pit.
Something
is starting that no one can
stop. I don't know which army will be
stronger, or how big the cannonballs will be. All I
can do is what Grandma hopes:
I can remember.

JAMES

I can't sleep. I keep thinking about that fight I had with Anikwa.
He had one rabbit in his hand—what about the other two? That "papa"

word he kept saying—is that the same word he said when he showed me
his fox pelt? Was he telling me a fox got my rabbits? Maybe he took

that last one so the fox wouldn't get it. Maybe . . . What's that smell?
What's all the noise out there? Smoke! I shake Ma and Pa awake, and Pa

runs out to see what's happening. He comes back in, red-faced, angry.
Lydia, he says, *it's the trading post! Maybe our house, too.* He grabs a bucket

and runs out. I start to follow. *No, James!* Ma says. *Stay here—you're too young.*
I can't stay in here while our house burns down! *Ma, I'm big enough,* I say.

I can carry water. She looks back and forth from me to the fire, scared of two
things at once. She takes a deep breath. *Go ahead,* she finally says. *Be careful.*

I find Pa in a line of men passing buckets from the pump to the trading post.
Go back insi— he begins, then looks from me to the fire and hands me a bucket.

ANIKWA

Rain Bird
is shaking my shoulder.
Wake up, she whispers, *I smell smoke!*
I sniff the air. *What's burning?*
Father and Mink are
still asleep, but
Grandma
comes in from outside.
When she opens the door, the smell
of smoke gets stronger. She wakes the others,
her voice low and sad. *It's happening,* she says. *One side
of the stockade. Our sister's house. The walls of the trading post
are falling. A few men chased all their animals into the forest
and they're shooting them with arrows as if they were
deer and elk. Those animals don't know how
to run and hide.* I think about their
birds—noisy chickens—
and about
the man
taking their eggs.
Who started the fire? I ask.
No one answers. Then Grandma says, *Grief
gathered kindling. Fear struck the flint.
Anger fans the flames.*

JAMES

In the morning, Ma, who never cries, is crying. Smoke burns my throat
like held-back tears. I swallow hard and go outside again to stand by Pa.

The pig, the cows, the hens, the rooster, and the goat are gone. We can't go out
to fish or hunt or set snares or pick berries. We're out of beans and oatmeal.

Pa, what will we eat? I try to make my voice sound normal, but it comes out
squeaky. Pa makes his own voice sound like he knows how to get food,

but all he says is, *We'll think of something.* If he had a real idea, he'd tell me.
We're standing here, looking at our burned-down house, not talking, when

I hear the sound of peepers on the other side of where the stockade gate
used to be. *Pa,* I say, *there's no peepers around here this time of year—I think*

that's Anikwa. At first, he doesn't know what I'm talking about, but then
he listens hard and says, *He shouldn't come so close, with the fire still smoldering.*

I think about it. *Pa,* I say, *he might be trying to help. Can I go see?* Pa answers, *No.*
Then he looks at the empty pasture. *Be quick,* he says, *and come straight back.*

ANIKWA

Good,
James heard me.
He's coming over to find out
what I want. He's looking
up and down, and all
around.
Aya,
I whisper.
He sees me. *Aya,*
he whispers back. I point to
the venison I brought, wrapped up
in a deerskin, hidden inside the hollow oak tree.
I point to him. His mouth falls open—he can't believe
we're giving it to them. He blinks back tears,
then picks up the meat and smiles big.
Thank you, he says. He repeats it
in Miami: *Neewe . . . niihka.*
I say the words Father
told me to say:
We did not start the fire.
James's face turns red. He looks like he's
thinking about something else, besides this meat.
Fox got my waapanswa, he says.
It wasn't you.

JAMES

Ma helps the cook fry up the meat, and all the men crowd in to get some.
My stomach hurts, but I try not to push. Ma puts her arm around me,

pulls me in, and serves me plenty. *Thank you, James,* she whispers.
She's not telling anyone where we got the meat—trying to protect me

and Anikwa. Mink and Wiinicia must have wrapped it in the deerskin.
I wonder why they gave us food. I tell Pa, *The Miami didn't start the fire.*

Pa says, *I hope that's true.* No one is sure of anything. Two soldiers went out
four days ago and just got back; they barely managed to run past everyone

outside the fort on their way in. What did they find out? *The Americans
are closer than the British, but we still don't know when either army will arrive.*

There's enough meat left for tomorrow. Maybe one more meal after that.
This is cooked the way I like it—juicy and hot, exactly the right amount of salt.

I hold it on my tongue—and the salty taste makes me ashamed. (Salt in the barrel,
pelts on the counter, empty salt scoop in my hand.) *Pa,* I say, *they need salt.*

ANIKWA

Wedaase
doesn't know we gave them meat.
Will James's family keep it for themselves,
or share it with the soldiers in the fort
so they'll all have enough
food to survive?
Either way,
I'm not sorry we helped.
About a hundred people in the fort, and
more than seven hundred gathered here in Kekionga,
surrounding them. Kwaahkwa agrees with Wedaase: *Let's*
attack now, while we outnumber them, before either army arrives.
Most of the young men agree. They take turns running
past the fort all day and all night, checking
to see if a sentry has fallen asleep.
So far no one has. I'm not old
enough to join them, but
I'm doing my part
by catching fish.
The ducks and geese
swim back and forth—they're
staying close to shore, quiet, as if they're
waiting with us, to see what
will happen next.

JAMES

The burned part of the stockade is still smoking. Pa grips my shoulder,
trying to hide us both behind a blackened post where our house used to be.

I point into the trees. *Over there, Pa. That's where Anikwa left the deer meat.*
We look down the trail, off to the side, up into the trees. We don't see anyone.

It's quiet. But that doesn't mean no one is around. *Too dangerous,* Pa says,
his hand still on my shoulder. He turns to go back into the fort. But we're

so close! If we just leave the salt here, Anikwa might not find it. I pull away
from Pa and run fast, to the hollow oak. Pa won't follow or shout after me;

he'll stay here watching, and if something happens, he'll help. But nothing
happens. I hide the salt in the tree, take out my whistle, and make the sound

of a blackbird. I listen closely. Not too far away, another blackbird answers.
I go back to Pa. We turn toward Ma, watching from a doorway in the fort.

When we get to her, she pulls us inside and asks, *Where was Anikwa hiding?
As soon as you left, he came out of nowhere, took the salt, and disappeared.*

SALT INSIDE THE WORDS

Salt on the tongue
the pleasure
of shared meals
the words
formed in our mouths
the taste of words
on their way
into the world:
salt inside the words.

ANIKWA

Most years, this is
my favorite season—when the corn
is almost ripe, I stand on a platform to scare off the birds.
Then we pick the golden ears, braid the husks
together, and hang the braided corn
to dry. In the evenings, I go
fishing, and Mink
and Grandma salt and dry the fish.
We store the corn and fish, and all the meat
and berries we have dried, so we'll have enough food
to last all winter. But this year we haven't had enough salt
to dry the fish, and the corn will not have time to ripen before
the armies get here. Everyone is working fast, staying up
late to bring in as much food as we can, but now these
hard questions: Can we feed all the people here,
and still have enough food for ourselves?
How much will the armies eat?
Where can we hide food so
they won't take it?
About ten more days—
that's how long we need for the corn
to fully ripen. But we won't have that long.
We have to find a way to hide
the food we have.

JAMES

Ma helps the cook find ways to make the deer meat last three days. They boil the bones for one last pot of soup. After this, there's no more food. Can't even

go out to the pump for water. Rupert says, *The American army could be here tomorrow.* Mr. Briggs: *Next day for sure.* When I see Mr. Briggs, I think of Isaac.

Wonder what he's doing right now. Molly throws her pinecone on the floor. I pick it up. She laughs, throws it down again. Wish I could be her age again.

Two soldiers try to guess how many men are in each army. *More Americans than British,* says one. *But how many Indians have joined the British?* asks the other.

When the American army gets here, will the soldiers know who's always lived in Kekionga, and who came here just to fight against them? How could they?

High in a tree, on a branch that hangs over the fort, a squirrel chatters at us. It's a real squirrel, not a tricky friend. *Shoot it, Pa,* I say. But he won't.

This whole place is like a tinderbox, he says. *A gunshot could set off the fighting.* I aim my slingshot. *No,* Pa says, *we don't know who might be hiding in that tree.*

ANIKWA

The armies
could be here tomorrow.
We sent a runner who has just returned,
bringing news that both armies
are almost here—and the
Americans are closer
than the British.
We had to pick the corn
too soon. It isn't dry. Where can we
hide it? Toontwa helps me dig holes to bury
what we can, but it's hard to cover them completely, and
if soldiers find these holes in the forest, they'll guess that food
is hidden in them. Rain Bird keeps on braiding corn faster
and faster, thinking hard. Now she looks up and offers
an idea: *Could we wrap our dried food and bury it*
under fire pits? If we make new fires, the ashes
will cover the holes—soldiers might not
think to look there. Everyone
stares at her. Grandma
smiles for the first time since we picked
the first ear of unripe corn. Now Rain Bird is wrapping
food as I put out our fire and start digging. Mink goes around
to all the families in Kekionga, telling everyone
Rain Bird's brilliant idea.

JAMES

Through the gap where the stockade burned down, we see people running
back and forth, around the fort. A lot of people. Kwaahkwa is the only one

I recognize. I'm looking for Anikwa or Old Raccoon, when I notice something:
it's almost all young men—no women or children. Not many older men.

Someone shoots a burning arrow toward the fort, and Mr. Briggs runs out
to stamp on it. Another arrow, not burning, flies toward him and barely

misses. He runs back to the fort. We're almost out of water—if another fire
starts, we won't have any way to quench it. Will we even have enough to drink?

Everything gets quiet. Five warriors go past, walking, not running, back
toward Kekionga. I see Kwaahkwa again—I want to run and ask him: *What*

is happening? Where's Anikwa? Old Raccoon? Are Rain Bird and Wiinicia safe?
But then he's gone. A hawk swoops in, kills a squirrel, and takes it to a tree.

After that, nothing happens for a while. No one comes near the fort. No more
flaming arrows. One flash of lightning in a blue-gray sky. Distant thunder.

ANIKWA

The elders talk all night,
and when the sun comes up, they've made
a hard decision: The American army is too big. The British
are too far away. There aren't enough of us. It's time
to leave, before this war begins.
Don't carry too much,
Mink says.
A fishing spear, a knife, a blanket.
Kwaahkwa is staying: *If we all leave, they'll think*
we're afraid. His mother's hardest questions and Rain Bird's
sweetest smiles haven't changed his mind. I'm almost as tall as he is.
Father, I say, *maybe I should stay here, too.* He rests his hand on my shoulder,
swallows hard, then asks, *Who would catch fish for everyone along the way?*
So now I can leave without shame. We pack a few canoes and horses,
but most of us are walking, going west to our relatives. They
will make room for us—it's what we always do—but we
don't want to eat the food they've gathered
for their own winter days. Father
picks up his fiddle,
sets it down. *Ready?* I ask Toontwa.
It's time to go. We circle around the fort in silence.
Inside, a baby cries—must be Molly. In the pond, a muskrat
watches us, dives deep—I wonder where
he will come up.

JAMES

No more lightning, but the thunder's louder. Ma tilts her head. *It's from the east,* she says, squeezing Molly so tight she busts out crying. We go out

to look. Is that a huge cloud on the horizon? Or dust rising from the road? *That's not thunder,* says Pa, *it's the army marching in.* The Americans are here.

The fort rings with cheers, and soldiers pour outside. Someone shoots a rifle into the sky. From the east another gunshot answers. Where's Pa going?

I start to follow him, but Ma holds me back. *No,* she says. *We don't know what will happen. You stay here.* She thinks I'm still a baby—makes me mad

and a little bit glad at the same time. The thunder sound comes closer as soldiers here line up to meet the army coming in. Isaac would be

cheering along with them—he'd know for sure which side he's on. I wish I did. Where is everyone from Kekionga? Are they getting ready

to start fighting? Old Raccoon didn't want a war, but he might fight in one if he has to. I listen for unusual birds or animals. No—I don't hear Anikwa.

ANIKWA

The morning sky
was still dark when we walked away
from Kekionga. The top branches of the oak tree
cradled the half-moon, and stars whispered
their sky-stories like old friends:
We will still be here
when you return.
Now the sun is high, the sky
is blue. Behind the steady song of *Cricket!*
Cricket! we hear thunder rumbling, but there's
no rain or lightning. *Stay quiet and listen,* Father says.
That's not thunder—the American army must be here. Toontwa
opens his eyes wide and stays close to my side. I tell him,
Not much farther. When we get to where siipiiwi goes in
two directions, we'll play tossball with our relatives.
I'll help you look for flints beside the water.
We walk all day, and arrive before
the sun sets, but we find
no friends, no cousins.
Cornfields stretch to the horizon,
some corn already picked, drying in the sun. Beans,
pumpkins, apples left in baskets say to us: *Welcome, friends.*
Rest here, please eat well. But why is no one here?
Where have they gone?

JAMES

Rupert made Molly a puppet on a stick that dances when I tap it on a board.
All morning I've been trying to keep her happy: tap, tap, tap—it dances, she

laughs, like everything's the same as usual. Ma wishes there were women
she could talk to, or someone to tell us what's happening, but we're stuck here

with the cook and a few soldiers who stayed to guard the fort. It's not as loud
as I thought a war would be. A few gunshots, a lot of hollering, another shot.

Soldiers we've never seen before come marching into the fort looking for food.
Cook shows them our supplies—that is, where the food would be if we had any.

The soldiers shake their heads and leave. Ma says it shouldn't be too long
before Pa can go out hunting—he'll get us a turkey, a goose, maybe a deer.

Pa made it clear that I can't leave the fort "until this is settled." *When will that be?*
I asked. *I don't know,* he answered. *It depends on where the British army is.*

Where are they? I look toward Kekionga. What's that, above the trees? Smoke—
fire! Houses burning. Whose houses? Flames rise high, then higher, wider.

ANIKWA

We eat our food,

not theirs. Grandma says, *Our friends*

and relatives will probably return tomorrow. No matter

where they've been, they'll come home hungry.

No one knows why everyone

has gone away from here.

As the sun goes down,

two people ride in at almost

the same time. First, from the north, a man

from this village returns to tell us they sent out a spy

who learned that the British turned back. If we decide to fight

the Americans, we will fight alone. They have five thousand men—

and even with all the warriors who are here now, we have

no more than fifteen hundred. A dark cloud crosses

Father's face. And then the second person

rides in from the east. At first,

I don't recognize this angry

red-faced man:

Kwaahkwa

has come to tell us, *I stayed*

out of sight and watched the army burn our longhouse,

all our homes—those made of cattail mats and those we've built with logs.

All our cornfields. Everything. Nothing left but ashes

where Kekionga was.

JAMES

All this smoke is choking me. What's going on? Pa comes in with food,
but not 'cause he went hunting. He puts it on the table—deer meat, corn,

maple sugar. And then a copper pot. The fiddle that belongs to Old Raccoon.
Pa, I ask, *who gave this to you?* He answers: *No one. They've all gone away.*

I took this from Old Raccoon's house before the soldiers set it on fire. Pa stole
from our friends? He slumps into a chair. Ma brings him water,

and we wait for him to tell us what's happening. Ma keeps coughing.
Her eyes are all red. Might be from the smoke, but it's also from crying.

Pa starts talking: *As far as I can tell, almost everyone in Kekionga left before
the army got here. Probably went to a village west of here. When the General*

*couldn't find anyone to fight, he said, "We'll make sure no one comes back later
to cause trouble."* Ma objects, *But most of the people in Kekionga don't even want*

to fight this war! Pa nods. *I know that. You know that. I couldn't stop them, Lydia.*
I ask, *How will they make new houses before winter?* Pa mutters, *That is the idea.*

ANIKWA

The cornfields here
go on and on, the wind blows
softly through them. Will we stay here with
our relatives this winter? We didn't bring
enough food. What kind of fish
can you catch here?
Father is quiet
for a long time. Then, as if he
hears the questions I'm not asking, he says,
I suppose they'll do for us what we do for others. When people
from the east are pushed west, we've always made room on our land.
What else can we do? So far, our fish and animals and cornfields have been enough
to feed us all. He stops talking for a minute. Then: *Tomorrow I'll show you*
a good fishing place not far from here. That should make me happy,
but the sadness in Father's voice is so deep and heavy
I can barely hear the words he speaks.
Gently, Grandma calls me
over to her.
Noohse,
will you go find some firewood?
Toontwa can help you. Good, I think, a chance
to explore, but then she adds, *Don't go farther than that oak tree—*
see it, at the edge of the clearing? If we call for you,
come quickly.

JAMES

I've never seen so many people in one place. They say there's five thousand
soldiers around here! Who can even count that high? Some of them seem

disappointed that the people they were going to fight went away before
they had a chance to fight them. The smoke from Kekionga settled down

by late last night, but when we woke up this morning, there was more of it!
Look at it all—dang! It's getting worse. Seems like the whole forest is on fire.

Pa comes storming in. *They're burning everything, from here down to the river!*
Ma gasps. I ask, *Why, Pa? There's not even any houses there!* Pa says, *Remember*

that day we took salt to Anikwa, and he hid somewhere, until he saw where we left it?
Not only that time—he always likes to hide. *Well,* says Pa, *they're trying to clear*

out any hiding places, so no one can sneak up and attack us. By burning everything?
Is that why those woodpeckers flew into the fort this morning, pecking holes

in the back wall? If someone burned down their trees, and all the nesting holes
they live in—they'd have to make new ones. Hey! What about the fox den?

ANIKWA

I'm awake
before the sun comes up. The river
here sounds different than it does in Kekionga.
A woodpecker hammers on a tree.
Kwaahkwa has been gone
all night, trying to
find out why
the people who live here
went away, and where they are. Now he
comes in and wakes his parents, and Grandma, Mink,
and Father. *Everyone has gone upriver,* he reports. *They say we
should go, too. No one thinks the army will stop at Kekionga.* He tells us
where the others are. We've been there before. It's near the riverbank,
where willows grow, their branches hanging down over the water.
We'll hide underneath them for a while. I imagine I can hear
the sound of distant voices. Soldiers paddling toward us.
Horses, wagons, an army like a marching forest.
(What are they eating?) I can almost
hear the gunfire,
see the flames. A great danger
close to us, and coming closer. Quickly,
we rouse everyone from sleep. Mothers keep
their babies quiet as we walk
into the cornfields.

JAMES

Fast as they marched in two days ago, the army's gone. Sixty soldiers
staying here to guard the fort. The rest—almost five thousand—marched

west and north this morning. The ground's all trampled everywhere.
Camps littered with scraps of animals they killed—they ate what they

were hungry for, leaving piles of hides and bones and guts all over.
The doe that had two fawns before comes up the hill with only one,

looking like she's asking me: *What happened? No grass to eat. No trees
to stand behind.* Where will the animals go? Will there be enough deer

for everyone to hunt next winter? *Pa,* I ask, *is the war over? What will
happen now?* He answers, *The British turned back. And then, as the Captain*

*put it: "When the Indians saw how bad they were outnumbered, they all
melted away into the forest."* Ma stands up and takes a long, deep breath,

like she's lifting something heavy, hard to carry. *How can we find out,* I ask,
what happened to everyone in Kekionga? She answers, *We will wait and see.*

ANIKWA

We walk between long rows
of corn until the sun is high above us.
Tall stalks swish like dancers as we pass. The corn
is sweet, ready to be picked; there's plenty
to eat when we get hungry. *Look,*
says Grandma, *how carefully*
they've planted it,
how beautifully it's grown.
We'll help them with the harvest, before
we go back home. A red-winged blackbird sings to us.
I answer it, as if this is an ordinary day—I'm just out walking
with my family. Rain Bird stays close to Kwaahkwa's mother. No one
knows where Kwaahkwa went. He said, *I'll meet you tomorrow night.*
He has his horse, and we're on foot, so he may arrive before us.
Now we've passed the cornfields, and we're on the trail
beside the river. A pair of herons fly in, land,
rest awhile, then take off, flying
east. When they're high
in the sky, I call:
What do you see? But I
don't understand their answer.
Rain Bird asks: *Are you sure you want to know*
what they see when they look back
at where we came from?

JAMES

Pa picks up his gun and heads out to see what's left of the forest. I follow
and he warns, *This won't be easy, James. I don't know what we'll find out there.*

I tell him I want to check the fox den. *It's not far—past the blackberry bushes,*
near the oak tree that got split by lightning—you know the one I mean? But wait—

the bushes and the tree aren't here. Where are we? Is that the rock I sit on,
to watch the trail for rabbits? It's hard to tell. Pa stomps along beside me.

What a waste, he says. *We have to rebuild our house, the stockade, the trading post—*
now we'll have to haul logs three times as far. They could have let us cut the trees

before they burned the underbrush. When we get to where the fox den was,
it's covered in ashes. A burned tree fell across the opening. At first I think

the foxes have all gone. Then, from under the blackened log, one peers out.
When I go up for a closer look, it tries to run away, but its leg's all busted up

so it can't walk. I lift the log—the fox snaps at my hand. *Stand back,* says Pa.
I have to do this, Son. And before I get his meaning, he shoots that fox dead.

ANIKWA

A tree root
poked into my back all night.
My damp blanket didn't keep me warm.
Is it already morning? No one slept.
We're quiet—waiting, listening,
sniffing the air, and asking,
Do you smell smoke?
Friends from a village north of us
arrive here, like we did two days ago, carrying
their blankets and a little food—enough to last a day or two.
Late afternoon and early evening, people come in from the south.
Grandma meets each group as they arrive. She speaks to the elders,
then tells us what she learns: *Everything is burned or burning.*
All the houses, cornfields, food they dried and couldn't hide
or bury. All the cattail mats they couldn't carry.
All the cornfields? The ones that took
a whole morning to walk
through? What about
the milkweed,
about to burst its seedpods?
The black-and-orange butterflies—thousands
of them, in a field of yellow flowers. I'm looking around at
all these people when Kwaahkwa comes riding in,
silent as a brewing storm.

JAMES

Stop that crying, Pa commands. I hiccup to a stop, clamp my mouth shut
to stop myself from yelling: *It didn't even bite me! We could've tamed it!*

We head for home. Can't get the picture of that fox out of my mind.
I don't tell Ma—I can't. But her face says she knows something's wrong.

Molly wakes up from her nap, crying worse than I did—no one yells at her
to stop it. Ma lifts her up and sings to her till she calms down, and then

she turns to me and asks, *What did you see this morning?* I tell her, *Lots of
burned-down trees.* That's all I have to say about it. But later on, when Pa's

not here, I say, *You know that deer we saw, with one fawn? She had two before.*
Ma nods. *I know the ones you mean. The missing fawn had a white patch*

on her leg. That's them. I take a deep breath. *We saw—a dead fox.* Dang.
Can't help it—I bust out crying. Ma says, *I heard a shot. It sounded like*

your father's gun. She knows. She puts Molly down, comes to me. Brushes
hair off my forehead, puts her hand on my shoulder. Leaves it there.

ANIKWA

Kwaahkwa
spreads his arms as wide
as they will reach, moves his fingers
up and down like flames,
his face like fire, too,
eyes wide open,
smoldering.
Father and the other
men have embers in their eyes
as they listen—what are they remembering?
Kwaahkwa leans in, drawing in the dirt: *Here,* he says,
and here. Here. And here. Stabbing a pointed stick into the ground
along a curvy line he's drawn to represent the river, he shows
us where the army burned each village, all the cornfields.
He points his stick at a spot between two villages.
Is he talking about my best fishing place?
I hid my horse and walked over
to the water's edge, close
to the herons' nest.
A heron flew out of a tree. I heard . . .
a shot. It fell in the water . . . and they . . . they left it there.
We stand with him in silence. I try to find words for my question:
Do the herons know the difference between them and us?
Grandma says, *Iihia. Yes. They do.*

JAMES

Pa and Ma are arguing. The American army went west for a few days; now they're here again, getting ready to head back east where they came from.

They'll be going through Piqua, and the women and children are ready to come home. Pa doesn't know where Old Raccoon and Piyeeto are,

so he volunteered to go to Piqua and bring everyone back home. Ma says, *No! How would we get along without you if . . .* She doesn't finish, but I know.

It's dangerous. Pa could get captured—or killed. After all that's happened, won't everyone be mad? *I can speak the languages along the way,* Pa says,

at least enough to ask for help. Ma says what I'm thinking: *What makes you so sure anyone will help you?* Pa answers, *If you were at Piqua . . .* Ma interrupts:

I'm not at Piqua! I'm here with James and Molly! And I don't want to stay in this fort any longer. When will you start cutting logs for our new house?

They go on like that, longer than I've ever heard them argue. I think Ma will win, but I fall asleep before she does, and when I wake up, Pa's not here.

ANIKWA

The sun

shines on a circle of white

hair, all the grandparents, talking to each other.

We have survived hard times before.

They talk all morning, then

all afternoon, on

into evening.

This comforts me.

They'll know what to do,

where we should go, how we can

stay together. But their faces, when they rise

from the circle, hold no answers, only sorrow. They've found

no way for us to stay together. Some will go to live with

relatives in other places, west or north or south.

Kwaahkwa's family is going so far west, we

don't know if we'll see them again.

Rain Bird turns her face away.

What will our family do?

Grandma's sister

lives six days' journey to the west.

But Father says, *If none of us return to Kekionga,*

they'll treat our home as if we have abandoned it. They'll say

we don't need it anymore. He looks at Grandma.

We will go back, they agree.

SALT STREAKS

Tears come from earth and sky,
from words moving through us.

We taste them as they fall,
leaving salt streaks on our faces.

We bear witness as they splash
back to earth, and are absorbed.

JAMES

I hate staying in the fort without Pa. Last night some of the soldiers
got in a big fight. Ma covered Molly's ears, but I heard the whole thing.

Those men miss their wives and children, Ma explained. *It won't be so bad
when things get back to normal.* But will that ever happen? How can it?

So far, none of the Miami have come back to Kekionga. I heard a soldier
say, *If they leave for good, I have a real nice place picked out for my house,*

*where the river curves around that big rock. Good fishing. The trees will
grow again, and we'll have shade.* I know the place he means, not far

from where Anikwa's house used to be—before it got burned down.
Ma won't let me go look. *When your pa gets home, we'll all go,* she says.

A few streaks of orange splash the evening sky, and pretty soon
it's red and purple. What's that sound? Quiet at first, then louder.

Sandhill cranes are flying in, hundreds of them, thousands.
Calling back and forth as they land in the burned cornfields.

ANIKWA

It's raining
as we begin our long walk home.
Soft rain, like the sky is crying, and it isn't going to stop.
The geese form into arrows pointing south, calling
down to us as they fly over. Cold, dark
days are coming. We won't
be ready for them.
I'm trying not to be so hungry,
not to think about the snow that will soon
cover the ground, how ice will slow the river to a stop.
The army's gone, but tracks are everywhere—grass and flowers
trampled down. Where are the animals? Did they kill them, or scare
them into hiding? Toontwa walks beside me. He's hungry too,
and since I don't have food to share, I tell him stories.
In one, I imitate the sound of sandhill cranes
and right then, hundreds of them fly
up from a burned cornfield—
there must be
a little corn
still left on the ground.
At the edge of the field, I see a deer, running.
Look, Toontwa—moohswa, I say. *See her white tail flashing?*
She stops and stands still for a minute
watching us.

JAMES

Ma keeps talking about her sister: *I wonder if Amanda could convince*
Ethan to leave Philadelphia. I hear it's getting crowded out east—

I'm sure there would be room for them here. Think of it, James!
She breaks into a big smile—the first one I've seen since Pa left.

You'd have cousins to play with! It's true, I'd like that. Uncle Ethan
could help us build our new house and then we'd help them build theirs.

I've never met my cousins, but I'd like to. Twin boys a little older than me,
a girl a year and a half younger. A boy about two years older than Molly.

With both families working together, Ma says, *we'd make the trading post*
bigger and better. We'll need new merchandise when we open it again,

and they have money—they could help replace what we lost in the fire.
She spends all day writing a letter. *I'll mail it when I can,* she says.

Rupert hears her talking and reminds us: *This part of the territory isn't open*
for settlement yet. They still have to work out some details in the treaties.

ANIKWA

It's almost dark
when we walk into Kekionga.
Or where it used to be. Now it's . . . ashes.
Kwaahkwa told us, but no one could
imagine how terrible it is:
every house
torn apart
and burned. The fish
we had to leave on drying racks
scattered everywhere, and trampled.
Corncobs and fish heads covered with flies—
the army must have eaten what they wanted, and then
destroyed whatever was left over. Didn't they know—
they must have known—it's too late to grow more
corn, and we won't be able to catch many
fish before the river freezes.
Will the animals find
their way
back?
Will deer give us
hides for warmth and shelter, meat
for winter food? Father says, *It's worse than I thought.*
Grandma says, *You helped them go to Piqua.*
They should help us now.

JAMES

I'm sitting on a rock near the burned-down trading post, trying out
a new tune on my whistle, when Old Raccoon walks up, holding

a white cloth on a stick to show he comes in peace. *Aya, James,* he says.
Hello, I answer. *You looking for Pa? He went to Piqua.* Ma sees us talking

and walks over. *Aya,* she says. *I expect Mr. Gray to be home tomorrow
or the next day.* Old Raccoon says, *I'll come back. Please tell him I need*

credit for tools and blankets. Ma says she'll tell him. I ask, *Will you bring
Anikwa next time you come?* Old Raccoon doesn't answer yes or no.

He looks at the charred ruins of our house. *We didn't start the fire,* he says.
Ma replies, *We know that.* She sweeps her arm toward Kekionga and says,

I'm sorry. There must be bigger words somewhere, but none of us
can find them. Old Raccoon turns away. As we watch him walking

down the trail, I remember how some people cheered when they saw
Kekionga burning. *What will they do now?* I ask. Ma has no answer.

ANIKWA

Soldiers found
the food we buried in the forest
but, as we hoped, they didn't think of looking
under fire pits. We dig through ashes, lift
out the food we hid, and carry it
to where we're building
our new wiikiaami.
Eleven other families
are making houses close to ours.
Later, we'll all work together, building
a new longhouse. We won't have time, before snow
falls, to build new homes with logs, but cattail walls and elk hides
will keep out the coldest winds. Grandma says, *This*
may be the hardest winter we have ever known.
But we will survive—we always have.
Here, where the river curves
around a rock that used
to stand in the shade
of seven maple
trees, my parents
and my grandparents are
buried. When summer comes again,
a cool breeze will blow across
their graves.

JAMES

When's Pa going to get back? Maybe then Ma will quit scrubbing
tables, floors, and walls. Not just the room we stay in—she's cleaning

the whole fort. *Take Molly outside?* she asks. Molly reaches out her hand
and smiles. I take her to the yard inside the fort, then out to where

the chickens used to be, and over to the garden to see if there's still
any food there. It's stripped clean except for a small patch of parsley.

I keep looking at the road from Piqua. Hey—is that them? Yes! Women,
children . . . and Pa is right behind them! I run back in the fort to tell Ma.

She splashes water on her face, like she's washing off the worry lines.
We go meet them—Pa swings down from his horse, hugs Ma and Molly,

roughs up my hair. *Looks like you took care of things around here, Son,* he says.
Isaac runs over. *Hey, James,* he hollers, *we won the war!* He looks at the burned

ground where the forest was: *Good job clearing out those bushes!* How come
seeing Isaac makes me feel more lonesome than I did when he was gone?

ANIKWA

Mink and Toontwa
are twisting strips of linden bark,
making twine to sew new cattail mats. Father and I dig
holes to set the sapling posts, while Grandma
teaches Rain Bird how to sew
the mats together. If we
keep on
working hard like this,
we'll have shelter by tomorrow night.
I hear someone coming—speaking English. James?
Yes. Mr. and Mrs. Gray, and Molly. They tie their horses to a tree.
Mr. Gray lifts down two big saddlebags, and looks around the clearing
till he sees us. We stop what we're doing. Mink glances at Grandma.
Rain Bird looks at me. What do they want? James looks around
with wide-open eyes. Hasn't he seen a family make a house
before? Grandma motions to them: *Come near the fire.*
James is holding something odd-shaped,
wrapped up in a blanket.
Father's fiddle.
He hands it to Father,
and Mr. Gray opens up a saddlebag,
takes out nine dried fish and a small bag of corn.
I saved what I could, he says. A gift—that was
ours to begin with.

JAMES

Anikwa looks at me like he's forgotten who I am, his eyes so sad
and angry I don't know what to say. I made him a new whistle, but now

it seems like it belongs someplace we can't go back to. I keep it
in my pocket. We give them a ball of twine, a new blade for their saw.

Ma says, *This is not on credit. It's a gift.* Pa looks surprised to hear that,
but he doesn't disagree. A few leaves are turning yellow, falling

from the trees into the river. When I do offer the whistle to Anikwa,
he takes it, but he doesn't smile. He looks older. He looks hungry.

They all do. Mink spreads out her hands and speaks to us. Old Raccoon
repeats her words in English: *Please sit with us and eat.* He goes away and

comes back with a roasted rabbit. Mink holds out a small gourd bowl to Pa.
He turns red and looks down at the ground before he dips his fingers in. Salt.

Thank you, he says softly. I whisper to Ma, *They hardly have any food. Why
are they feeding us?* She answers, *You should know by now. This is who they are.*

ANIKWA

If we
sit down to eat with James
and his family, will he and I be able to play
a song together on our whistles?
That's what he hopes for,
the question I see
in his eyes:
Are you still my friend?
Last night Father said, *There will be*
more settlers. Everyone who is here now will invite
friends and relatives from the places they came from themselves.
Soon there will be more of them than us, and they will tell us where
we can and cannot live. Is it already too late to prevent that?
I listen to the river, to the fire at the center of our circle,
two coyotes howling back and forth, and people
talking softly as they make a wiikiaami.
I keep listening until I find my own
music, and then I lift
the whistle
to my mouth and play.
Father joins in on his fiddle; James
adds a tune that moves in and out of ours. We send
our music out into the darkening sky
and let the river carry it.

NOW THE SUGAR MAPLE

Now the sugar maple
draws water through deep roots
up into branches.
Deer come to lick a wound
scraped into bark,
taste the tree's sap seeping out.
More deer gather.
As they once led us to salt,
now they show us
how to find this small sweet taste,
moving up and out
into new buds, each branch
offering to sky
a gift of light and shadow.

NOTES
Form
Salt
Names

GLOSSARY OF MIAMI ⟨MYAAMIA⟩ WORDS

ACKNOWLEDGMENTS

NOTES

Form

Anikwa's poems are shaped like patterns of Miami ribbon work, a traditional art form created by sewing different colors of ribbons in patterns layered on top of each other to form diamond and triangle shapes. James's poems began as an image of the stripes on an American flag. As I discovered the two voices, the pulse-like shape of Anikwa's poems wove through the horizontal lines of James's poems, and the two voices created something new that held the story as it opened out.

Poems about salt are placed throughout the story to allow readers to pause between one event and another.

Salt

People and animals everywhere need salt. In 1812, it was used in food preservation as well as being eaten for flavor and health. The poems about salt tell how it was formed, discovered, and used in the place known as Myaamionki, the land of the Miami.

Names

As far as I know, these are not the names of real people, living now or in the past. I am grateful to Miami friends who helped me name the fictional characters; we agreed that it was best not to try to follow the complex traditions of Miami naming, and that some of the characters would be known by English translations of their Miami names.

Miami Name	Meaning in English
Anikwa (ah-NIK-wah)	squirrel
Eehsipana (ay-SIP-ah-nah)	Old Raccoon
Kwaahkwa (KWAHK-wah)	pileated woodpecker
Piitilaanoonhsa (pee-tih-lah-NOON-sah)	cliff swallow or "Rain Bird"
Šinkohsa (shing-GOH-sah)	Mink
Toontwa (TOON-dwa)	bullfrog
Wiinicia (wee-NICH-ya)	box turtle

Names in other languages*	Meaning in English
Shawnee	
Piyeeto (pee-yay-TOH)	He Brings It
Ojibwe	
Waaseechkang (wah-SAYCH-kahng)	Brings In Light
Ottawa	
Wedaase (weh-DAH-say)	Warrior

*Suggested by tribal members who speak each of these languages

GLOSSARY OF MIAMI ⟨MYAAMIA⟩ WORDS

To listen to these words (and many more) spoken by Miami speakers, go to the online Miami dictionary: myaamiadictionary.org

Miami (Myaamia)	Meaning in English
amehkwa (ah-MEH-kwa)	beaver
aya (EYE-yah)	hello, greeting
iihia (EE-hyah)	yes
kiihkoneehsa (kee-ko-NAY-sa)	fish
maalhseenhsi (mahl-SAYN-si)	pocketknife
makiinkweemina (mah-king-gway-MI-nah)	blackberry
makiinkweeminiiki (mah-king-gway-mi-NEE-ki)	blackberries
mihši-maalhseensa (MI-shi-mahl-SAYN-zah)	American boy
mihši-neewe (MI-shi-NAY-weh)	thank you very much
miililo (mee-li-LO)	give it to me
moohci (MOO-chi)	no
moohswa (MOOS-wah)	deer
myaamiinse (miahm-MEEN-zeh)	Miami child
Myaamionki (miahm-mee-OHNG-gi)	land of the Miami
neewe (NAY-weh)	thank you
niihka (NEE-kah)	friend
noohse (NOO-seh)	grandchild
paapankamwa (PAH-pahng-GAM-wah)	fox

siipiiwi (see-PEE-wi)   river

waapanswa (wah-PAHN-zwah)   rabbit

wiihkapaakani (weeh-KAH-pah-   salt
   KAH-ni)

wiikiaami (wee-kee-YAH-mi)   house

ACKNOWLEDGMENTS

I've been learning about this history for over twenty years, and could never thank everyone who has helped me discover and write the story, but I will mention some people and organizations without whom the book could not have been written.

Friends in the Miami Tribe of Oklahoma and the Miami Nation of Indiana have always been helpful and encouraging. Special thanks to George Ironstrack, Laura Nagy, Scott Shoemaker, George Strack, Dani Tippmann, and all the children, parents, grandparents, teachers, and counselors at the Miami Language and Culture camps. Warm gratitude to Catherine Nagy for her suggestion to "end it with music."

Mihši-neewe to the Myaamia Center (myaamiacenter.org), at Miami University, in Oxford, Ohio—a source of maps, language, and historical and cultural information.

I thank the children I knew in Telida, Alaska, in the early 1980s, adults now, who answered such questions as "How long can you leave a rabbit in a snare?" My friendship with their parents, grandparents, and great-grandparents also finds a place in this story.

Thanks to Reta Sands and Howard Kimewon, who suggested names for the Ottawa and Ojibwe characters.

A number of scholars generously offered their expertise. I thank Ted Bartlett, chemist; Tim McCoy, geologist; and Daryl Baldwin, David Costa, and Chad Thompson, linguists.

I found helpful historical resources at the Allen County Public Library; the IPFW Helmke Library; the Allen County–Fort Wayne Historical Society; the Eteljorg Museum; and OYATE. Special thanks to historians John Beatty, Todd Pelfrey, Stuart Rafert, Clifford Scott, Peggy Seigel, and Eric Vosteen.

Although I have not named the historical figures who were important in the events this story portrays, I would like to acknowledge one person whose name often came up in my research. Angeline Chapeteau Peltier was a peacemaker in her time, and an inspiration and comfort to me as I imagined my story.

I am grateful for financial support from the National Endowment for the Arts, and the Eugene and Marilyn Glick Foundation.

Thank you to the Authors Guild and the Society of Children's Book Writers and Illustrators, especially the Indiana listserve and the Fort Wayne writers group.

Karen Baldwin, Monica Edinger, Carol Roberts, and Margaret Steen offered helpful comments, as did young readers Julia Beatty, Zachary Herbert, and Clark and Harrison Webster. Thank you.

Thanks to Ketu Oladuwa, Sox Sperry, and Lisa Tsetse, who have shared a profound interest in this story for many years. To other friends who encourage me in so many ways: you know who you are—I appreciate you.

Many thanks to my editor, Frances Foster: what a privilege to work together on this, our seventh book. I also appreciate Susan Dobinick, Karla Reganold, Jay Colvin, and others at FSG and Macmillan, and Ginger Knowlton at Curtis Brown.

I have a large and rather amazing extended family—thanks, everyone! And a big thank-you to Chad, Lloyd, and Glen, whose suggestions are always thoughtful, specific, and helpful. I couldn't be luckier.